D0382206

SWEET TALK

....
....
....
....
....
....
....
....
....
....
....
....

STEPHANIE VAUGHN

Sweet

TALK

RANDOM HOUSE   NEW YORK

Published in the United States by Random House, Inc., New York and
simultaneously in Canada by Random House of Canada Limited, Toronto.

Some stories in this work were originally published in *The New Yorker*
and *Redbook*.
"Sweet Talk," "Other Women," and "The Architecture of California"
were originally published in *Antaeus* magazine.

Library of Congress Cataloging-in-Publication Data
Vaughn, Stephanie.
Sweet talk / by Stephanie Vaughn.
p.   cm.
ISBN 0-394-57605-5
I. Title.
PS3572.A934S94   1990
813'.54—dc20   89-42773

Manufactured in the United States of America
24689753
First Edition

BOOK DESIGN BY LILLY LANGOTSKY

For

MARGUERITE IRENE ROGERS VAUGHN

and in memory of

LOUISA DOUGLAS ROGERS

and

FRANCIS MERLE VAUGHN

ACKNOWLEDGMENTS

For support of this project, I wish to thank the Ohio Arts Council, the Copernican Society, and the National Endowment for the Arts. In particular, I wish to thank the members of the United States Congress who voted to create and maintain the National Endowment for the Arts, especially Senator Howard Metzenbaum of Ohio and Senator Daniel Moynihan of New York.

For reading the manuscript again and again—and for his sense of humor and big heart—I thank the Clam Man, Michael Claude Ignatius Quilmer Koch.

CONTENTS

SWEET TALK

....
....
....
....
....
....
....
....
....
....
....

ABLE, BAKER, CHARLIE, DOG

*W*hen I was twelve years old, my father was tall and awesome. I can see him walking across the parade ground behind our quarters. The wind blew snow into the folds of his coat and made the hem swoop around his legs. He did not lower his head, he did not jam his hands into the pockets. He was coming home along a diagonal that would cut the parade ground into perfect triangles, and he was not going to be stopped by any snowstorm. I stood at the kitchen door and watched him through a hole I had rubbed in the steamy glass.

My grandmother and mother fidgeted with pans of food that had been kept warm too long. It was one o'clock on Saturday and he had been expected home at noon.

"You want to know what this chicken looks like?" said my grandmother. "It looks like it died last year."

My mother looked into the pan but didn't say anything.

My grandmother believed my mother should have

married a minister, not an Army officer. Once my mother had gone out with a minister, and now he was on the radio every Sunday in Ohio. My grandmother thought my father had misrepresented himself as a religious man. There was a story my mother told about their first date. They went to a restaurant and my father told her that he was going to have twelve sons and name them Peter, James, John, et cetera. "And I thought, Twelve sons!" said my mother. "Boy, do I pity your poor wife." My mother had two miscarriages and then she had me. My father named me Gemma, which my grandmother believed was not even a Christian name.

"You want to know what this squash looks like?" said my grandmother.

"It'll be fine," said my mother.

Just then the wind gusted on the parade ground, and my father veered to the left. He stopped and looked up. How is it possible you have caught me off guard, he seemed to ask. Exactly where have I miscalculated the velocities, how have I misjudged the vectors?

"It looks like somebody peed in it," my grandmother said.

"Keep your voice low," my father told me that day as we ate the ruined squash and chicken. "Keep your voice low and you can win any point."

We were living in Fort Niagara, a little Army post at the juncture of the Niagara River and Lake Ontario. We had been there through the fall and into the winter, as my father, who was second in command, waited for his next promotion. It began to snow in October. The arctic winds swept across the lake from Canada and shook the windows of our house. Snow drifted across the parade ground, and floes of ice piled up against each other in the river, so that if a person were courageous enough, or foolhardy enough, and also lucky, he could walk the mile across the river to Canada.

"And always speak in sentences," he told me. "You have developed a junior-high habit of speaking in fragments. Learn to come to a full stop when you complete an idea. Use semicolons and periods in your speech."

My mother put down her fork and knife. Her hands were so thin and light they seemed to pass through the table as she dropped them in her lap. "Zachary, perhaps we could save some of the lecture for dessert?" she said.

My grandmother leaned back into her own heaviness. "The poor kid never gets to eat a hot meal," she said. She was referring to the rule that said I could not cut my food or eat while I was speaking or being spoken to. My father used mealtimes to lecture on the mechanics of life, the how-tos of a civilized world. Normally I was receptive to his advice, but that day I was angry with him.

"You know, Dad," I said, "I don't think my friends are going to notice a missing semicolon."

I thought he would give me a fierce look, but instead he winked. "And don't say 'you know,' " he said.

He never said "you know," never spoke in fragments, never slurred his speech, even years later when he had just put away a fifth of scotch and was trying to describe the Eskimo custom of chewing up the meat before it was given to the elders, who had no teeth. He spoke with such calculation and precision that his sentences hung over us like high vaulted ceilings, or rolled across the table like ornaments sculptured from stone. It was a huge cathedral of a voice, full of volume and complexity.

He taught me the alphabet. Able, Baker, Charlie, Dog. It was the alphabet the military used to keep *b*'s separate from *v*'s and *i*'s separate from *y*'s. He liked the music of it, the way it sounded on his fine voice. I was four years old and my grandmother had not come to live with us yet. We were stationed in Manila, and living in a house the Army had built on squat stilts to protect us from the insects. There was a typhoon sweeping inland, and we could hear the hoarse sound of metal scraping across the Army's paved street. It was the corrugated roof of the house next door.

"Don't you think it's time we went under the house?" my mother said. She was sitting on a duffel bag that contained our tarps and food rations. The house had a loose plank in the living-room floor, so that if the roof blew away, or the walls caved in, we could escape through the opening and sit in the low space between the reinforced floor and the ground until the military rescue bus came.

My father looked at me and said, "Able, Baker, Charlie, Dog. Can you say it, Gemma?"

I looked up at the dark slope of our own metal roof.

"Can you say it?"

"Able, Baker, Charlie, Dog," I said.

The metal rumbled on the road outside. My mother lifted the plank.

"We will be all right," he said. "Easy, Fox, George, How."

"Anybody want to join me?" said my mother.

"Easy."

"Rachel, please put that plank back."

"Easy, Fox, George, How," I said.

My mother replaced the plank and sat on the floor beside me. The storm grew louder, the rain fell against the roof like handfuls of gravel.

"Item, Jig, King." My father's voice grew lower, fuller. We sat under the sound of it and felt safe. "Love, Mike, Nan."

But then we heard another sound—something that went *whap-whap,* softly, between the gusts of rain. We tilted our heads toward the shuttered windows.

"Well," said my father, standing up to stretch. "I think we are losing a board or two off the side of the house."

"Where are you going?" said my mother. "Just where do you think you're going?"

He put on his rain slicker and went into the next room. When he returned, he was carrying a bucket of nails and a hammer. "Obviously," he said, "I am going fishing."

We moved back to the States when I was six, and he taught me how to play Parcheesi, checkers, chess, cribbage, dominoes, and twenty questions. "When you lose," he told me, "don't cry. When you win, don't gloat."

He taught me how to plant tomatoes and load a shotgun shell. He showed me how to gut a dove, turning it inside out as the Europeans do, using the flexible breastbone for a pivot. He read a great many books and never forgot a fact or a technical description. He explained the principles of crop rotation and the flying buttress. He discussed the Defenestration of Prague.

When I was in elementary school, he was sent abroad twice on year-long tours—once to Turkey and once to Greenland, both strategic outposts for America's Early Warning System. I wanted to, but I could not write him letters. His came to me every week, but without the rhythms of his voice the words seemed pale and flat, like the transparent shapes of cells under a microscope. He did not write about his work, because his work was secret. He did not send advice, because that he left to my mother and grandmother in his absence. He wrote about small things—the smooth white rocks he found on a mountainside in Turkey, the first fresh egg he ate in Greenland. When I reread the letters after he died, I was struck by their grace and invention. But when I read them as a child, I looked through the words—"eggs . . . shipment . . . frozen"—and there was nothing on the other side but the great vacuum of his missing voice.

"I can't think of anything to say," I told my mother the first time she urged me to write to him. He had already been in Turkey for three months. She stood behind me at the heavy library table and smoothed my hair, touched my shoulders. "Tell him about your tap lessons," she said. "Tell him about ballet."

"Dear Dad," I wrote. "I am taking tap lessons. I am also taking ballet." I tried to imagine what he looked like. I tried to put a face before my face, but it was gray and featureless, like the face of a statue worn flat by wind and rain. "And I hope you have a Happy Birthday next month," I concluded, hoping to evade the necessity of writing him again in three weeks.

The autumn I turned twelve, we moved to Fort Niagara, which was the administrative base for the missile sites strung along the Canadian border between Lake Erie and Lake Ontario. It was a handsome post, full of oak trees, brick buildings, and history. The French had taken the land from the Indians and built the original fort. The British took the fort from the French, and the Americans took it from the British. My father recounted the battles for us as we drove there along the wide sweep of the Niagara River, past apple orchards and thick pastures. My grandmother sat in the back seat and made a note of each red convertible that passed. I was supposed to be counting the white ones. When we drove through the gate and saw the post for the first time—the expanses of clipped grass, the tall trees, the row of Colonial houses overlooking the river—my grandmother put down her tablet and said, "This is some post." She looked at my father admiringly, the first indication she had ever given that he might be a good match for my mother after all. She asked to be taken to the far end of the post, where the Old Fort was. It sat on a point of land at the juncture of the lake and river, and looked appropriately warlike, with its moat and tiny gun windows, but it was surprisingly small—a simple square of yellow stone, a modest French château. "Is this all there is?" I said as my grandmother and I posed for pictures on the drawbridge near two soldiers dressed in Revolutionary War costumes. It was hard to imagine that chunks of a vast continent had been won and lost within the confines of a fortress hardly bigger than Sleeping Beauty's castle at Disneyland. Later, as we drove back along the river, my father said in his aphoristic way, "Sometimes the biggest battles are the smallest ones."

The week after we settled in our quarters, we made the obligatory trip to the Falls. It was a sultry day—

Indian summer—and our eyes began to water as we neared the chemical factories that surrounded the city of Niagara Falls. We stopped for iced tea and my father explained how the glaciers had formed the escarpment through which the Falls had cut a deep gorge. *Escarpment*—that was the term he used, instead of *cliff*. It skidded along the roof of his mouth and entered the conversation with a soft explosion.

We went to the Niagara Falls Museum and examined the containers people had used successfully to go over the Falls early in the century, when there was a thousand-dollar prize given to survivors. Two were wooden barrels strapped with metal bands. One was a giant rubber ball reinforced with a steel cage. A fourth was a long steel capsule. On the walls were photographs of each survivor and plaques explaining who had been injured and how. The steel capsule was used by a man who had broken every bone in his body. The plaque said that he was in the hospital for twenty-three weeks and then took his capsule around the world on a speaking tour. One day when he was in New Zealand, he slipped on an orange peel, broke his leg, and died of complications.

We went next to Goat Island and stood on the open bank to watch the leap and dive of the white water. My

mother held her handbag close to her breasts. She had
a habit of always holding things this way—a stack of
dinner plates, the dish towel, some mail she had brought
in from the porch; she hunched over slightly, so that her
body seemed at once to be protective and protected. "I
don't like the river," she said. "I think it wants to
hypnotize you." My father put his hands in his pockets
to show how at ease he was, and my grandmother went
off to buy an ice-cream cone.

At the observation point, we stood at a metal fence
and looked into the frothing water at the bottom of the
gorge. We watched bits and pieces of rainbows appear
and vanish in the sunlight that was refracted off the
water through the mist. My father pointed to a black
shape in the rapids above the Horseshoe Falls. "That's
a river barge," he said. He lowered his voice so that he
could be heard under the roar of the water. "A long time
ago, there were two men standing on that barge waiting
to see whether in the next moment of their lives they
would go over."

He told us the story of the barge then—how it had
broken loose from a tug near Buffalo and floated down-
river, gathering speed. The two men tore at the air,
waved and shouted to people on shore, but the barge
entered the rapids. They bumped around over the rocks,

and the white water rose in the air. One man—"He was the thinking man," said my father—thought they might be able to wedge the barge among the rocks if they allowed the hull to fill with water. They came closer to the Falls—four hundred yards, three hundred—before the barge jerked broadside and stopped. They were there all afternoon and night, listening to the sound of the water pounding into the boulders at the bottom of the gorge. The next morning they were rescued, and one of the men, the thinking man, told the newspapers that he had spent the night playing poker in his head. He played all the hands, and he bluffed himself. He drew to inside straights. If the barge had torn loose from the rocks in the night, he was going to go over the Falls saying, "Five-card draw, jacks or better to open." The other man sat on the barge, his arms clasped around his knees, and watched the mist blow back from the edge of the Falls in the moonlight. He could not speak.

"The scream of the water entered his body," said my father. He paused to let us think about that.

"Well, what does that mean?" my grandmother said at last.

My father rested his arms on the fence and gazed pleasantly at the Falls. "He went insane."

The river fascinated me. I often stood between the yellow curtains of my bedroom and looked down upon it and thought about how deep and swift it was, how black under the glittering surface. The newspaper carried stories about people who jumped over the Falls, fourteen miles upriver from our house. I thought of their bodies pushed along the soft silt of the bottom, tumbling silently, huddled in upon themselves like fetuses—jilted brides, unemployed factory workers, old people who did not want to go to rest homes, teenagers who got bad grades, young women who fell in love with married men. They floated invisibly past my bedroom window, out into the lake.

That winter, I thought I was going to die. I thought I had cancer of the breasts. My mother had explained to me about menstruation, she had given me a book about the reproductive systems of men and women, but she had not told me about breasts and how they begin as invisible lumps that become tender and sore.

I thought the soreness had begun in a phys. ed. class one day in December when I was hit in the chest with a basketball. I didn't worry about it, and it went away by New Year's. In January, I found a pamphlet at the bus stop. I was stamping my feet in the cold, looking down at my boots, when I saw the headline—CANCER: SEVEN WARNING SIGNALS. When I got home, I went into the bathroom and undressed. I examined myself for enlarged moles and small wounds that wouldn't heal. I was systematic. I sat on the edge of the tub with the pamphlet by my side and began with my toenails, looking under the tips of them. I felt my soles, arches, ankles. I worked my way up my body and then I felt the soreness again, around both nipples. At dinner that night I didn't say anything all through the meal. In bed I slept on my back, with my arms stiff against my sides.

The next Saturday was the day my father came home late for lunch. The squash sat on the back of the stove and turned to ocher soup. The chicken fell away from the bones. After lunch he went into the living room and drank scotch and read a book. When I came down for supper, he was still sitting there, and he told my mother he would eat later. My grandmother, my mother, and I ate silently at the kitchen table. I took a long bath. I scrubbed my chest hard.

I went straight to my bedroom, and after a while my mother came upstairs and said, "What's wrong?"

I didn't say anything.

She stood in front of me with her hands clasped in front of her. She seemed to lean toward her own hands. "But you've been acting, you know"—and here she laughed self-consciously, as she used the forbidden phrase—"you know, you've been acting different. You were so quiet today."

I went to my chest of drawers and took the pamphlet out from under a stack of folded underpants and gave it to her.

"What's this?" she said.

"I think I have Number Four," I said.

She must have known immediately what the problem was, but she didn't smile. She asked me to raise my nightgown and she examined my chest, pressing firmly, as if she were a doctor. I told her about the soreness. "Here?" she said. "And here? What about here, too?" She told me I was beginning to "develop." I knew what she meant, but I wanted her to be precise.

"You're getting breasts," she said.

"But I don't *see* anything."

"You will."

"You never told me it would hurt."

"Oh, dear. I just forgot. When you're grown up you just forget what it was like."

I asked her whether, just to be safe, I could see a doctor. She said that of course I could, and I felt better, as if I had had a disease and already been cured. As she was leaving the room, I said, "Do you think I need a bra?" She smiled. I went to sleep watching the snow fall past the window. I had my hands cupped over my new breasts.

. . .

When I awoke, I did not recognize the window. The snow had stopped and moonlight slanted through the glass. I could not make out the words, but I heard my father's voice filling up the house. I tiptoed down the back staircase that led to the kitchen and stood in the slice of shadow near the doorjamb. My grandmother was telling my mother to pack her bags. He was a degenerate, she said—she had always seen that in him. My mother said, "Why, Zachary, why are you doing this?"

"Just go pack your bags," my grandmother said. "I'll get the child."

My father said conversationally, tensely, "Do I have to break your arms?"

I leaned into the light. He was holding on to a bottle of scotch with one hand, and my mother was trying to pull it away with both of hers. He jerked his arm back and forth, so that she was drawn into a little dance, back and forth across the linoleum in front of him.

"The Lord knows the way of righteousness," said my grandmother.

"Please," said my mother. "Please, please."

"And the way of the ungodly shall perish," said my grandmother.

"Whose house is this?" said my father. His voice exploded. He snapped his arm back, trying to take the bottle from my mother in one powerful gesture. It smashed against the wall, and I stepped into the kitchen. The white light from the ceiling fixture burned across the smooth surfaces of the refrigerator, the stove, the white Formica countertops. It was as if an atom had been smashed somewhere and a wave of radiation was rolling through the kitchen. I looked him in the eye and waited for him to speak. I sensed my mother and grandmother on either side of me, in petrified postures. At last, he said, "Well." His voice cracked. The word split in two. "Wel-el." He said it again. His face took on a flatness.

"I am going back to bed," I said. I went up the narrow steps, and he followed me. My mother and grandmother came along behind, whispering. He tucked in the covers, and sat on the edge of the bed, watching me. My mother and grandmother stood stiff against the door. "I am sorry I woke you up," he said finally, and his voice was deep and soothing. The two women watched him go down the hall, and when I heard his steps on the front staircase I rolled over and put my face in the pillow. I heard them turn off the lights and say good-night to me. I heard them go to their bedrooms. I lay there for a long time, listening for a sound downstairs, and then it came—the sound of the front door closing.

I went downstairs and put on my hat, coat, boots. I followed his footsteps in the snow, down the front walk, and across the road to the riverbank. He did not seem surprised to see me next to him. We stood side by side, hands in our pockets, breathing frost into the air. The river was filled from shore to shore with white heaps of ice, which cast blue shadows in the moonlight.

"This is the edge of America," he said, in a tone that seemed to answer a question I had just asked. There was a creak and crunch of ice as two floes below us scraped each other and jammed against the bank.

"You knew all week, didn't you? Your mother and your grandmother didn't know, but I knew that you could be counted on to know."

I hadn't known until just then, but I guessed the unspeakable thing—that his career was falling apart— and I knew. I nodded. Years later, my mother told me what she had learned about the incident, not from him but from another Army wife. He had called a general a son of a bitch. That was all. I never knew what the issue was or whether he had been right or wrong. Whether the defense of the United States of America had been at stake, or merely the pot in a card game. I didn't even know whether he had called the general a son of a bitch to his face or simply been overheard in an unguarded moment. I only knew that he had been given a 7 instead of a 9 on his Efficiency Report and then passed over for promotion. But that night I nodded, not knowing the cause but knowing the consequences, as we stood on the riverbank above the moonlit ice. "I am looking at that thin beautiful line of Canada," he said. "I think I will go for a walk."

"No," I said. I said it again. "No." I wanted to remember later that I had told him not to go.

"How long do you think it would take to go over and back?" he said.

"Two hours."

He rocked back and forth in his boots, looked up at the moon, then down at the river. I did not say anything.

He started down the bank, sideways, taking long, graceful sliding steps, which threw little puffs of snow in the air. He took his hands from his pockets and hopped from the bank to the ice. He tested his weight against the weight of the ice, flexing his knees. I watched him walk a few yards from the shore and then I saw him rise in the air, his long legs scissoring the moonlight, as he crossed from the edge of one floe to the next. He turned and waved to me, one hand making a slow arc.

I could have said anything. I could have said "Come back" or "I love you." Instead, I called after him, "Be sure and write!" The last thing I heard, long after I had lost sight of him far out on the river, was the sound of his laugh splitting the cold air.

In the spring he resigned his commission and we went back to Ohio. He used his savings to invest in a chain of hardware stores with my uncle. My uncle arranged the contracts with builders and plumbers, and supervised the employees. My father controlled the inventory and handled the books. He had been a logistics officer, and all the skills he might have used in supervising the movement of land, air, and sea cargoes, or in calculating the disposition of several billion dollars' worth of military supplies, were instead brought to bear on the deployment of nuts and bolts, plumbers' joints and nipples, No. 2 pine, Con-Tact paper, acrylic paint, caulking guns, and rubber dishpans. He learned a new vocabulary—traffic builders, margins, end-cap displays, perfboard merchandisers, seasonal impulse items—and spoke it with the ostentation and faint amusement of a man who has just mastered a foreign language.

"But what I really want to know, Mr. Jenkins," I heard him tell a man on the telephone one day, "is why you think the Triple Gripper Vegetable Ripper would make a good loss-leader item in mid-winter." He had been in the hardlines industry, as it was called, for six months, and I was making my first visit to his office, and then only because my mother had sent me there on the pretext of taking him a midmorning snack during a busy Saturday. I was reluctant to confront him in his civilian role, afraid I would find him somehow diminished. In fact, although he looked incongruous among the reds, yellows, and blues that the previous owner had used to decorate the office, he sounded much like the man who had taught me to speak in complete sentences.

"Mr. Jenkins, I am not asking for a discourse on coleslaw."

When he hung up, he winked at me and said, "Your father is about to become the emperor of the building-and-housewares trade in Killbuck, Ohio."

I nodded and took a seat in a red-and-blue chair.

Then he looked at his hands spread upon the spotless ink blotter and said, "Of course, you know that I do not give a damn about the Triple Gripper Vegetable Ripper."

I had skipped a grade and entered high school. I saw less and less of him, because I ate dinner early so that I could go to play rehearsals, basketball games, dances. In the evenings he sat in a green chair and smoked cigarettes, drank scotch, read books—the same kinds of books, year after year. They were all about Eskimos and Arctic explorations—an interest he had developed during his tour in Greenland. Sometimes, when I came in late and was in the kitchen making a snack, I watched him through the doorway. Often he looked away from the book and gazed toward the window. He would strike a match and let it burn to his thumb and fingertip, then wave it out. He would raise the glass but not drink from it. I think he must have imagined himself to be in the Arctic during those moments, a warrior tracking across the ice for bear or seal. Sometimes he was waiting for me to join him. He wanted to tell me about the techniques the Eskimos had developed for survival, the way they stitched up skins to make them watertight vessels. He became obsessive on the subject of meat. The Eskimo diet was nearly all protein. "Eat meat," he said. Two professors at Columbia had tested the value of the Eskimo diet by eating nothing but caribou for a year and claimed they were healthier at the end of the experiment than they had been before.

Later, when I went to college, he developed the

habit of calling me long distance when my mother and grandmother had gone to bed and he was alone downstairs with a drink. "Are you getting enough protein?" he asked me once at three in the morning. It was against dorm rules to put through calls after midnight except in cases of emergency, but his deep, commanding voice was so authoritative ("This is Gemma Jackson's father, and I must speak with her immediately") that it was for some time believed on my corridor that the people in my family were either accident-prone or suffering from long terminal illnesses.

He died the summer I received my master's degree. I had accepted a teaching position at a high school in Chicago, and I went home for a month before school began. He was overweight and short of breath. He drank too much, smoked too many cigarettes. The doctor told him to stop, my mother told him, my grandmother told him.

My grandmother was upstairs watching television and my mother and I were sitting on the front porch. He was asleep in the green chair, with a book in his lap. I left the porch to go to the kitchen to make a sandwich, and as I passed by the chair I heard him say, "Ahhhh.

Ahhhhh." I saw his fist rise to his chest. I saw his eyes open and dilate in the lamplight. I knelt beside him.

"Are you okay?" I said. "Are you dreaming?"

We buried him in a small cemetery near the farm where he was born. In the eulogy he was remembered for having survived the first wave of the invasion of Normandy. He was admired for having been the proprietor of a chain of excellent hardware stores.

"He didn't have to do this," my mother said after the funeral. "He did this to himself."

"He was a good man," said my grandmother. "He put a nice roof over our heads. He sent us to Europe twice."

Afterward I went alone to the cemetery. I knelt beside the heaps of wilting flowers—mostly roses and gladiolus, and one wreath of red, white, and blue carnations. Above me, the maple pods spun through the sunlight like wings, and in the distance the corn trumpeted green across the hillsides. I touched the loose black soil at the edge of the flowers. Able, Baker, Charlie, Dog. I could remember the beginning of the alphabet, up through Mike and Nan. I could remember the end. X-ray, Yoke, Zebra. I was his eldest child, and he taught me what he knew. I wept then, but not because he had gone back to Ohio to read about the Eskimos and sell

the artifacts of civilized life to homeowners and builders. I wept because when I was twelve years old I had
stood on a snowy riverbank as he became a shadow on
the ice, and waited to see whether he would slip between
the cracking floes into the water.

*S*ometimes Sam and I loved each other more when we were angry. "Day," I called him, using the surname instead of Sam. "Day, Day, Day!" It drummed against the walls of the apartment like a distress signal.

"Ah, my beautiful lovebird," he said. "My sugar-sweet bride."

For weeks I had been going through the trash trying to find out whether he had other women. Once I found half a ham sandwich with red marks that could have been lipstick. Or maybe catsup. This time I found five slender cigarette butts.

"Who smokes floral-embossed cigarettes?" I said. He had just come out of the shower, and droplets of water gleamed among the black hairs of his chest like tiny knife points. "Who's the heart-attack candidate you invite over when I'm out?" I held the butts beneath his nose like a small bouquet. He slapped them to the floor and we stopped speaking for three days. We moved through the apartment without touching, lay stiffly in

separate furrows of the bed, desire blooming and wither-
ing between us like the invisible petals of a night-bloom-
ing cereus.

We finally made up while watching a chess tournament on television. Even though we wouldn't speak or
make eye contact, we were sitting in front of the sofa
moving pieces around a chess board as an announcer
explained World Championship strategy to the viewing
audience. Our shoulders touched but we pretended not
to notice. Our knees touched, and our elbows. Then we
both reached for the black bishop and our hands
touched. We made love on the carpet and kept our eyes
open so that we could look at each other defiantly.

We were living in California and had six university
degrees between us and no employment. We lived on
food stamps, job interviews, and games.

"How many children did George Washington, the
father of our country, have?"

"No white ones but lots of black ones."

"How much did he make when he was commander
of the Revolutionary Army?"

"He made a big to-do about refusing a salary but
later presented the first Congress with a bill for a half
million dollars."

"Who was the last slave-owning president?"

"Ulysses S. Grant."

We had always been good students.

It was a smoggy summer. I spent long hours in air-conditioned supermarkets, touching the cool cans, feeling the cold plastic stretched across packages of meat. Sam left the apartment for whole afternoons and evenings. He was in his car somewhere, opening it up on the freeway, or maybe just spending time with someone I didn't know. We were mysterious with each other about our absences. In August we decided to move east, where a friend said he could get us both jobs at an unaccredited community college. In the meantime, I had invented a lover. He was rich and wanted to take me to an Alpine hotel, where mauve flowers cascaded over the stone walls of a terrace. Sometimes we drank white wine and watched the icy peaks of mountains shimmer gold in the sunset. Sometimes we returned to our room carrying tiny ceramic mugs of schnapps that had been given to us, in the German fashion, as we paid for an expensive meal.

In the second week of August, I found a pair of red lace panties at the bottom of the kitchen trash.

I decided to tell Sam I had a lover. I made my lover into a tall, blue-eyed blond, a tennis player on the circuit, a Phi Beta Kappa from Stanford who had offers from the movies. It was the tall blond part that needled Sam, who was dark and stocky.

"Did you pick him up at the beach?" Sam said.

"Stop it," I said, knowing that was a sure way to get him to ask more questions.

We were wrapping cups and saucers in newspaper and nesting them in the slots of packing boxes. "He was taller than you," I said, "but not as handsome."

Sam held a blue-and-white Dresden cup, my favorite wedding present, in front of my eyes. "You slut," he said, and let the cup drop to the floor.

"Very articulate," I said. "Some professor. The man of reason gets into an argument and he talks with broken cups. Thank you, Alexander Dope."

That afternoon I failed the California driver's test again. I made four right turns and drove over three of the four curbs. The highway patrolman pointed out that if I made one more mistake I was finished. While daydreaming, I drove through a red light.

On the way back to the apartment complex, Sam squinted into the flatness of the expressway and would not talk to me. I put my blue-eyed lover behind the wheel. He rested a hand on my knee and smiled as he drove. He was driving me west, away from the Vista View Apartments, across the thin spine of mountains that separated our suburb from the sea. At the shore there would be seals frolicking among the rocks and starfish resting in tidal pools.

"How come you never take me to the ocean?" I said. "How come every time I want to go to the beach I have to call up a woman friend?"

"If you think you're going to Virginia with me," he said, "you're dreaming." He eased the car into our numbered space and put his head against the wheel. "Why did you have to do it?"

"I do not like cars," I said. "You know I have always been afraid of cars."

"Why did you have to sleep with that fag tennis player?" His head was still against the wheel. I moved closer and put my arm around his shoulders.

"Sam, I didn't. I made it up."

"Don't try to get out of it."

"I didn't, Sam. I made it up." I tried to kiss him. He let me put my mouth against his, but his lips were unyielding. They felt like the skin of an orange. "I didn't, Sam. I made it up to hurt you." I kissed him again and his mouth warmed against mine. "I love you, Sam. Please let me go to Virginia."

" 'George Donner,' " I read from the guidebook, " 'was sixty-one years old and rich when he packed up his family and left Illinois to cross the Great Plains, the desert, and the mountains into California.' " We were driving through the Sierras, past steep slopes and the deep shade of an evergreen forest, toward the Donner Pass, where in 1846 the Donner family had been trapped by an early snowfall. Some of them died and the rest ate the corpses of their relatives and their Indian guides to survive.

"Where are the bones?" Sam said, as we strolled past glass cases at the Donner Pass Museum. The cases were full of wagon wheels and harnesses. Above us a recorded voice described the courageous and enterprising spirit of American pioneers. A man standing nearby with a young boy turned to scowl at Sam. Sam looked at him and said in a loud voice, "Where are the bones of the people they ate?" The man took the boy by the hand and started for the door. Sam said, "You call this American history?" and the man turned and said, "Listen, mister, I can get your license number." We laughed about that as we descended into the plain of the Great Basin desert in Nevada. Every few miles one of us would say the line and the other one would chuckle, and I felt as if we had been married fifty years instead of five, and that everything had turned out okay.

. . .

Ten miles east of Reno I began to sneeze. My nose ran and my eyes watered, and I had to stop reading the guidebook.

"I can't do this anymore. I think I've got an allergy."

"You never had an allergy in your life." Sam's tone implied that I had purposefully got the allergy so that I could not read the guidebook. We were riding in a secondhand van, a lusterless, black shoebox of a vehicle, which Sam had bought for the trip with the money he got from the stereo, the TV, and his own beautifully overhauled and rebuilt little sports car.

"Turn on the radio," I said.

"The radio is broken."

It was a hot day, dry and gritty. On either side of the freeway, a sagebrush desert stretched toward the hunched profiles of brown mountains. The mountains were so far away—the only landmarks within three hundred miles—that they did not whap by the windows like signposts, they floated above the plain of dusty sage and gave us the sense that we were not going anywhere.

"Are you trying to kill us?" I said when the speedometer slid past ninety.

Sam looked at the dash surprised and, I think, a little pleased that the van could do that much. "I'm getting hypnotized," he said. He thought about it for another mile and said, "If you had managed to get your license, you could do something on this trip besides blow snot into your hand."

"Don't you think we should call ahead to Elko for a motel room?"

"I might not want to stop at Elko."

"Sam, look at the map. You'll be tired when we get to Elko."

"I'll let you know when I'm tired."

We reached Elko at sundown, and Sam was tired. In the office of the Shangri-la Motor Lodge we watched another couple get the last room. "I suppose you're going to be mad because I was right," I said.

"Just get in the van." We bought a sack of hamburgers and set out for Utah. Ahead of us a full moon rose, flat and yellow like a fifty-dollar gold piece, then lost its color as it rose higher. We entered the Utah salt flats, the dead floor of a dead ocean. The salt crystals glittered like snow under the white moon. My nose stopped running, and I felt suddenly lucid and calm.

"Has he been in any movies?" Sam said.

"Has who been in any movies?"

"The fag tennis player."

I had to think a moment before I recalled my phantom lover.

"He's not a fag."

"I thought you made him up."

"I did make him up but I didn't make up any fag."

A few minutes later he said, "You might at least sing something. You might at least try to keep me awake." I sang a few Beatles tunes, then Simon and Garfunkel, the Everly Brothers, and Elvis Presley. I worked my way back through my youth to a Girl Scout song I remembered as "Eye, Eye, Eye, Icky, Eye, Kai, A-nah." It was supposed to be sung around a campfire to remind the girls of their Indian heritage and the pleasures of surviving in the wilderness. "Ah woo, ah woo. Ah woo knee key chee," I sang. "I am now five years old," I said, and then I sang, "Home, Home on the Range," the song I remembered singing when I was a child going cross-country with my parents to visit some relatives. The only thing I remembered about that trip besides a lot of going to the bathroom in gas stations was that there were rules that made the traveling life simple. One was: Do not hang over the edge of the front seat to talk to your mother or father. The other was: If you have to throw up, do it in the blue coffee can; the red one is full of cookies.

"It's just the jobs and money," I said. "It isn't us, is it?"

"I don't know," he said.

A day and a half later we crossed from Wyoming into Nebraska, the western edge of the Louisiana Purchase, which Thomas Jefferson had made so that we could all live in white, classical houses and be farmers. Fifty miles later the corn arrived, hundreds of miles of it, singing green from horizon to horizon. We began to relax and I had the feeling that we had survived the test of American geography. I put away our guidebooks and took out the dictionary. *Matachin, mastigophobia, matutolypea.* I tried to find words Sam didn't know. He guessed all the definitions and was smug and happy behind the wheel. I reached over and put a hand on his knee. He looked at me and smiled. "Ah, my little buttercup," he said. "My sweet cream pie." I thought of my Alpine lover for the first time in a long while, and he was nothing more than mist over a distant mountain.

In a motel lobby near Omaha, we had to wait in line for twenty minutes behind three families. Sam put his arm around me and pulled a tennis ball out of his jacket. He bounced it on the thin carpet, tentatively, and when he saw it had enough spring, he dropped into an exaggerated basketball player's crouch and ran across the lobby. He whirled in front of the cigarette machine and passed the ball to me. I snagged it and threw it back. Several people had turned to stare at us. Sam winked at them and dunked the ball through an imaginary net by the wall clock, then passed the ball back to me. I dribbled around a stack of suitcases and went for a lay-up by a hanging fern. I misjudged and knocked the plant to the floor. What surprised me was that the fronds were plastic but the dirt was real. There was a huge mound of it on the carpet. At the registration desk, the clerk told us that the motel was already full and that he could not find our names on the advance reservation list.

"Nebraska sucks eggs," Sam said loudly as we carried our luggage to the door. We spent the night curled up on the hard front seat of the van like boulders. The bony parts of our bodies kept bumping as we turned and rolled to avoid the steering wheel and dash. In the morning, my knees and elbows felt worn away, like the peaks of old mountains. We hadn't touched each other sexually since California.

"So she had big ta-ta's," I said. "She had huge ta-ta's and a bad-breath problem." We had pushed on through the corn, across Iowa, Illinois, and Indiana, and the old arguments rattled along with us, like the pots and dishes in the back of the van.

"She was a model," he said. He was describing the proprietress of the slender cigarettes and red panties.

"In a couple of years she'll have gum disease," I said.

"She was a model and she had a degree in literature from Oxford."

I didn't believe him, of course, but I felt the sting of his intention to hurt. "In a few years, she'll have emphysema."

"What would this trip be like without the melody of your voice," he said. It was dark, and taillights glowed on the road ahead of us like flecks of burning iron. I remembered how, when we were undergraduates attending different colleges, he used to write me letters that said: Keep your skirts down and your knees together, don't let anyone get near your crunch. We always amused each other with our language.

"I want a divorce," I said in a motel room in Columbus, Ohio. We were propped against pillows on separate double beds watching a local program on Woody Hayes, the Ohio State football coach. The announcer was saying, "And here in front of the locker room is the blue-and-gold mat that every player must step on as he goes to and from the field. Those numbers are the score of last year's loss to Michigan." This was just before the famous coach was fired for trying to punch a Clemson football player during a nationally televised game. There are still people in Ohio who remember Woody Hayes with such fondness that they will tell you that that Clemson player was actually reaching down with his neck to hit the coach's hand. I was saying, "Are you listening? I said I want a divorce when we get to Virginia."

"I'm listening."

"Don't you want to know why I want a divorce?"

"No."

"Well, do you think it's a good idea or a bad idea?"

"I think it's a good idea."

"You do?"

"Yes."

The announcer said, "And that is why the night before the big game Woody will be showing his boys reruns of the film *Patton.*"

That night someone broke into the van and stole everything we owned except the suitcases we had with us in the motel room. They even stole the broken radio. We stood in front of the empty van and looked up and down the row of parked cars as if we expected to see another black van parked there, one with two pairs of skis and two tennis rackets slipped into the spaces between the boxes and the windows.

"I suppose you're going to say I'm the one who left the door unlocked," I said.

Sam sat on the curb. He sat on the curb and put his head into his hands. "No," he said. "It was probably me."

The policeman who filled out the report tried to write "Miscellaneous Household Goods" on the clip-boarded form, but I made him list everything I could remember, as the three of us sat on the curb—the skis and rackets, the chess set, a baseball bat, twelve boxes of books, two rugs that I had braided, an oak bed frame Sam had refinished. I inventoried the kitchen items: two bread pans, two cake pans, three skillets. I mentioned every fork and every measuring cup and every piece of bric-a-brac I could recall—the trash of our life, suddenly made valuable by the theft. When the policeman had left without giving us any hope of ever recovering our things, I told Sam I was going to pack and shower. A half hour later when I came out with the suitcases, he was still on the curb, sitting in the full sun, his cotton shirt beginning to stain in wing shapes across his shoulder blades. I reached down to touch him and he flinched. It was a shock—feeling the tremble of his flesh, the vulnerability of it, and for the first time since California I tried to imagine what it was like driving with a woman who said she didn't want him, in a van he didn't like but had to buy in order to travel to a possible job on the other side of the continent, which might not be worth reaching.

On the last leg of the trip, Sam was agreeable and compliant. If I wanted to stop for coffee, he stopped immediately. If I wanted him to go slower in thick traffic, he eased his foot off the pedal without a look of regret or annoyance. I got out the dictionary. *Operose, ophelimity, ophryitis.* He said he'd never heard of any of those words. Which president died in a bathtub? He couldn't remember. I tried to sing to keep him company. He told me it wasn't necessary. I played a few tunes on a comb. He gazed pleasantly at the turnpike, so pleasantly that I could have made him up. I could have invented him and put him on a mountainside terrace and set him going. "Sammy," I said, "that stuff wasn't much. I won't miss it."

"Good," he said.

Then I said, "It was Harding who died in the tub."

About 3 A.M. green exit signs began to appear announcing the past and the future: Colonial Williamsburg, Jamestown, Yorktown, Patrick Henry Airport. "Let's go to the beach," I said. "Let's just go all the way to the edge of the continent." It was a ludicrous idea.

"Sure. Why not."

He drove on past Newport News and over an arching bridge toward Virginia Beach. We arrived there just at dawn and found our way into a residential neighborhood full of small pastel houses and sandy lawns. "Could we just stop right here?" I said. I had an idea. I had a plan. He shrugged as if to say what the heck, I don't care, and if you want to drive into the ocean that will be fine, too.

We were parked on a street that ran due east toward the water—I could see just a glimmer of ocean between two hotels about a mile away. "All right," I said, with the forced, brusque cheerfulness of a high-school coach. "Let's get out and do some stretching exercises." Sam sat behind the wheel and watched me touch my toes. "Come on, Sammy. Let's get loose. We haven't done anything with our bodies since California." He yawned, got out of the van, and did a few arm rolls and toe touches. "All right now," I said. "Do you think a two-block handicap is about right?" He had always given me a two-block advantage during our foot races in California. He yawned again. "How about a one-and-a-half-block lead, then?" He crossed his arms and leaned against the van, watching me. I couldn't tell whether he had nodded, but I said anyway, "I'll give you a wave when I'm ready." I walked down the middle of the street past houses that had towels hanging over porch rails and toys lying on front walks. Even a mile from the water, I smelled the salt and seaweed in the air. It made me feel light-headed and for a moment I tried to picture Sam and myself in one of those houses with tricycles and toilet trainers and small latched gates. We had never discussed having a child. When I turned to wave, he was still leaning against the van.

I started out in a jog, then picked up the pace, and hit what seemed to be about the quarter-mile mark doing a fast easy run. Ahead of me the stretch of water between the two hotels was undulating with gold. I listened for the sound of Sam's footsteps but heard only the soft taps of my own tennis shoes. The sea drew closer and the sky above it fanned out in ribs of orange and purple silk. I was afraid to look back. I was afraid that if I turned to see him, Sam might recede forever into the damp gray of the western sky. I slowed down in case I had gone too fast and he wanted to catch up. I concentrated on the water and listened to the still, heavy air. By the time I reached the three-quarters mark, I realized that I was probably running alone.

I hadn't wanted to lose him.

I wondered whether he had waited by the van or was already headed for Newport News. I imagined him at a phone booth calling another woman collect in California, and then I realized that I didn't actually know whether there was another woman or not. For a wild moment I hoped there was and that she was rich and would send him money. I had caught my second wind and was breathing easily. I looked toward the shore without seeing it and was sorry I hadn't measured the distance and thought to clock it, since now I was running against time and myself, and then I heard him— the unmistakable sound of a sprint and the heavy, whooping intake of his breath. He passed me just as we crossed the main street in front of the hotels, and he reached the water twenty feet ahead of me.

"Goddammit, Day," I said. "You were on the grass, weren't you?" We were walking along the hard, wet edge of the beach, breathing hard. "You were sneaking across those lawns. That's a form of cheating." I drummed his arm lightly with my fists pretending to beat him up. "I slowed down because I thought you weren't there." We leaned over from the waist, hands on our hips, breathing toward the sand. The water rolled up the berm near our feet and flickered like topaz.

"You were always a lousy loser," he said.

I said, "You should talk."

WE'RE ON TV IN THE UNIVERSE

*M*y theory of the universe is that it's not moving outward from a Big Bang nor collapsing backward into the center. It's moving back and forth, breathing in and out, just like lungs. Sometimes, when the universe is running uphill, it breathes faster, and the stars from our vantage point in the Milky Way whip left and right like windshield wipers. The universe, when it is in deep sleep at five o'clock in the morning, has a heartbeat of 124 beats per minute, the same heartbeat that an unhatched chicken has just before it begins to crash its head against the shell.

Last winter I wrecked my car during an ice storm on Interstate 17. I had a chicken in a cage on the front seat beside me. I had the cage strapped in with the passenger seat belt, and a towel draped over the cage, so that the chicken wouldn't have to look at the weather. I was on my way to a party, and I was wearing my only party outfit, a black satin dress with a giant silver belt that was actually a music box in disguise—when you pressed the buckle, it played "Stars and Stripes Forever." The chicken was actually a young rooster who hadn't yet learned his own music. When he tried to crow a cock-a-doodle-do, he made a horrible scraping metal sound that came out "er-err-errr." It was early evening, black and snowy, the roadbed hissing beneath my tires, the chicken going "er-err-errr" every so often beneath the towel.

"So you don't want to go to a party?" I said to the chicken. I knew by then that I was driving on a chancy road, and I was trying to keep myself going with the chicken talk. "So you don't want to party?" I said. "You want to go back home and become drumsticks and Hot Buffalo Wings?"

"Er-err-errr," the chicken said.

"Just kidding," I said. The chicken was going to be a present for a man who lived in the country and owned ducks, geese, and a swan. One thing I knew about this man was that he liked his birds the way some people like dogs and cats, and he probably wouldn't eat them. I was trying to picture the chicken in his new home when I crossed a bridge over the Susquehanna and encountered the silence of black ice. The tires lost their hiss, the chicken shut up, and about fifty yards after I hit the ice, I hit a Tioga County Sheriff's Department car. The car was parked on the road berm just beyond the bridge, and inside the car a sheriff was radioing for a tow truck, as if he knew I was coming and that when I got there, our two cars were going to need help.

My car did a kind of simple dance step down the highway on its way to meet the sheriff's car. It threw its hips to the left, it threw its hips to the right, left, right, left, right, then turned and slid, as if it were making a rock-and-roll move toward the arms of a partner.

Before the impact, when my car was still grace on ice, when my car was no longer in touch with the planet but now sliding above a thin layer of air and water, four thousand pounds of chrome and steel, bronze metallic paint, power steering, power brakes, AC, AM/FM, good tires, fine upholstery, all the things you like to see in an ad when you're looking for a big, used American car, when it was gliding through that galaxy of flashing lights, on its way through Andromeda, Sirius, and the Crab Nebula, it crossed my mind that surely it was against the laws of physics to hit a patrol car. If you were sliding above ice, you might hit a regular car, or a pole, or a fence, or an asteroid, but you could not hit the car of a man with a badge, a gun, bulletproof windows, citation forms in his pocket, handcuffs, the power to arrest you, a man working hard on a bad night.

Just about all of those things did really fly through

my head and, recognizing the impossibility of the event, as my car slid sideways toward the side of the other car, I felt weightless and invisible. I felt harmless and happy.

Even for a sheriff, Officer Mike Cook was very tall. Officer Cook was linebacker tall, he was Jack-and-the-Beanstalk tall, he was as tall as my desire to be back home. Looking up at him, at the black silhouette of his hat, at the crazed lights on the top of his car slinging snowfish around his head, I lost contact with my native language. He put his hands on his hips and waited. When he perceived that words for me were as ephemeral as snowflakes, he said in his deep patrolman's voice, his made-for-TV-voice, "We're not having a very good evening, are we?"

We, he said. Officer Cook had embraced me with his pronoun.

It was then that I knew I loved Officer Cook, the blackness of his huge wet boots, the tenderness of his large hands as he lighted the flares and placed them along the roadside. People died that night on Interstate 17, and we were alive. We were alive! I loved Officer Cook for having survived the double whump of my car smashing into his car, nose to tail, and tail to nose, and then having thought of something to say about it afterward. We hit him twice, the chicken and I, before we spun out again heading back down the road in the direction we had been going before the accident. It took me a moment to realize that we were still moving and that the wheels had caught their traction again and needed an application of the brakes.

"Is it over?" I said to the chicken. When I lifted the towel, he was walking in small circles around the cage, looking for an escape perhaps. Poor creature, who in the early A.M. that day had been a resident of Old MacDonald's Pet Shop eating yellow corn and practicing his ridiculous crow in front of cooing children.

The reason Officer Cook had been radioing for a tow truck was that another car had already hit the ice slick and had departed from the road. It had slid down a steep bank and been caught by drifts. The owner was standing now on the safe side of the guard rail waiting for the truck. He was a juggler, a college kid who had just driven four hundred miles on his way home from a Springsteen concert.

"I'm only twenty miles from home," he said.

"Me too," I said. "Twenty miles from home and ten miles from a big party."

He had three snowballs and was tossing them in the air as we talked. He tossed them so high that they disappeared into the feathered darkness before they met his lightning hands again.

"You want a ride home?" he said. "Your car's done for the night." In fact, my car was going to need three thousand dollars in body work plus the four-hundred-dollar transmission job I had been postponing, and therefore it was done forever. I looked down at his red Mustang held by snow.

"How do you know *your* car's not done for the night?"

"My car didn't hit a police car," he said.

I don't know why the TV crew didn't put the juggler in the picture, maybe because they believed that the real story lay in the irony of a patrolman's needing help. The crew arrived breathlessly, a van from a station in Binghamton. One of them had a video camera, and the other did the talking. Officer Cook, who was back in his car talking on the radio, got out in order to say, "We don't want any more vehicles on this roadside. Move along now."

Traffic was moving very slowly past us in the far lane, cars, an eighteen-wheel rig, their drivers invisible behind black glass, straining to see us, I imagined, our little tableau, a cautionary tale.

"How many cars involved here?" the TV man said.

"Three," Officer Cook said, turning to get in his car.

"Anybody hurt? Anybody injured?"

"I don't think so," Officer Cook said. "Get off the road," he said, and slammed his door.

Just then I leaned against the car so that I could prop my elbows on the roof, and my belt buckle broke into "Stars and Stripes Forever." The TV man turned and took me in for the first time and then noticed the juggler, who by then was throwing five snowballs into the air and was all concentration.

"Did you hit the cop, or did he hit you?"

"I hit him," I said. I could see the TV man thinking about it—here were a juggler in the snow, a cop with a wrecked car, and a woman who sounded like a brass band, maybe there was a story here—and then he shook his head no.

"Let's get out of here," he said to his cameraman.

They jogged to the van, and before they got in I heard the TV man say, "I know there's a better wreck somewhere down the road."

I looked at the juggler, who dropped his hands and let the balls fall past him like tiny comets. "You fail the wreck test," he said. "They're looking for an A-plus wreck. They're looking for something with bodies."

The belt had arrived at the piccolo section of the march, the silvery shooting-star solo of the brave little instrument soaring above the heavy brass ones. The juggler and I paused to listen to it. We tapped our feet in the slush and kept time with our bodies. When the march was over, the juggler said, "Nice belt."

The happiest person I met that night was the tow-truck driver. She was making lots of money in the bad weather and knew how to handle the roads. "My policy is people first and then their wrecks," she told us. "You might have some aches and pains, or your feet might be froze." So we got in the cab, the juggler, the chicken, and I, and rode one mile to the exit and a gas station, where we waited for the tow truck to bring in our cars. Officer Cook had to stay behind and wait for a policeman to come and fill out an accident report. That was the last I saw of him until the eleven o'clock news.

At the station, there were already three other drivers waiting for their cars. We all still had that adrenaline high you get from a close call, and we kept taking turns describing our accidents. We kept embellishing as we went, so that the accidents got more frightening as we added the sounds of breaking glass (my taillights) and the screech of metal (the juggler's bumper scraping the end of the guardrail), things you hear but don't listen to when the car is still moving. Someone wanted to know if I was a veterinarian. In the spirit of the moment, I said, "Not exactly," and they all looked skeptical—We're all truth-tellers here, they seemed to say. "Actually, this is a birthday present for a veterinarian who lives in the country," I said. That was true enough to make sense of where I was and how I happened to arrive there with a live chicken. I played John Philip Sousa for them. The juggler juggled some soda cans. We asked him what the hardest things were to juggle and he said, "Live lobsters." A famous juggler in New York City had tried live lobsters once on a dare from someone in the audience, but the lobsters kept snapping at him. The chicken drank some water from a paper cup and, feeling more himself again, began to speak his peculiar chicken language.

In the end, I didn't accept a ride home with the juggler, because I had decided he was probably doing a little speed. Instead, I took a room at Koch's Universe Motel, which had a giant neon sign depicting stars and spaceships. I gave the chicken to the tow-truck driver. She had three children who wanted a pet, and she was the only one at the gas station who promised she wouldn't eat it. At eleven o'clock I got a glimpse of Officer Cook on TV. The camera panned over his car, pausing at the crushed front fender and the popped hood. Then it cut to him just long enough for him to say, "We don't want any more vehicles on this roadside," and then the report hurried on to the "better wrecks." Just before Officer Cook got to the word "roadside," I got a hazy look at myself in the background, separated from Officer Cook by the hood of his car and streaks of falling snow. There we were, together again. There we were, the two of us locked forever in the frame of a TV screen, bouncing off of satellites and caroming over the planet. We were still going places. We were leading off the transmission from earth in front of sports and weather, the late-night talk shows, and old movies. We were going to be up there with everybody who had ever been on TV. Truman and Eisenhower, JFK and LBJ. You name it. Pete Rose and Gloria Steinem. We were moving fast, already on our way to the moon. Pretty soon we'd be passing through the orbit of Mars, then Jupiter, Saturn, Uranus, Neptune, and Pluto. We'd be going to Andromeda and who knows where else. What a vacation.

A confession now. What was I doing on the road with a live chicken and a musical belt? I was going to a party where I imagined that I would be noticed as an interesting person. The Poultry Woman. The Marching

Band Woman. A woman you would like to discover at a party. There were going to be famous people at that party, Watkins Glen race drivers, glass sculptors from Corning, writers from New York City, maybe even athletes and actors. I was between jobs again and living alone. When I set out in bad weather I had a feeling. Something was going to change for me that night, something that was going to relocate me in the universe. Watching television in the motel, I thought about it. I was right. Something happened.

*M*y mother cannot say the word *cancer.* A year ago, after an operation to remove a tumor at the juncture of her small and large intestines, she used the word *blockage* to explain what the problem had been. "The doctors have found a blockage in my intestines," she told relatives who came to visit as she convalesced on the porch. "Now that it's gone, I can finally eat again, thank God."

My Aunt Ruda took me aside and said, "I want you to tell me the truth about your mother. Is she talking about an ulcer, or what?" Aunt Ruda is my mother's sister-in-law. When I visit every summer, at the end of my teaching year, she has a new inventory of details about other people's medical problems—grotesque incisions, ruined arteries, fatal blood clots, irradiated wombs. Aunt Ruda is overweight, fat with the stories of other people's grief.

"Gemma, you mustn't tell anyone what the operation was really for," my mother said to me, and I saw the fear skate across her eyes, cold in the blue light of the kitchen's fluorescent bulb. "If any of your aunts and uncles find out that it was something really serious, they'll keep asking how I am." I understood then how a question about one's health can be like a sheath on a sword, hiding the real question: "When will you die?"

Now my mother and I visit as we always have the first night I am home in Ohio. We sit in front of the television in separate chintz-covered chairs, our feet propped on a shared footstool, a box of chocolate butter-creams on the table between us. This year, however, I have come home early to deal with what my mother says is a "new wrinkle." For one year, she has led a healthy, normal life. She has gained weight, she has bought new clothes. She has visited me in California. But two weeks ago, during a quarterly checkup, something unexpected appeared in the X rays.

"You look healthy," I tell her. "You look wonderful."

"I feel fine," she says. "I can eat anything."

We invent a dessert menu for the next week. Chocolate mousse, peach Melba, apple spice cake, banana cream pie, cherries in cognac. In the muted light of the television screen, in the old hollows of familiar furniture, we feel protected.

. . .

Usually in June there is a milky haze lying among the wooded hills and the steaming crops—young corn, ripe wheat, silvery middle-aged oats. Today, the landscape surprises us with its sparkle and clarity, as if we have driven into the center of a crystal prism. I can see the way a slender leaf of corn ripples along its center vein. I can see the fanning seed head on a stalk of yellow wheat.

"Ironwort, tiger lily." My mother gives me back names from my youth, identifying the wildflowers that lean frailly away from the edge of the road.

When I was a child, I suffered from frequent kidney infections, which my mother called "attacks." It was not until years later, when I casually used the term during a college physical examination, that I recognized its benign absurdity. "An attack?" said the doctor. "A kidney *attack*?" At once, I saw the image it must have called up, of a scowling cartoon kidney, with thin arms and mitten-shaped hands carrying muggers' weapons. Now we drive back through the Ohio countryside. We are on our way home from the university hospital, where a second opinion has been offered on the spot that showed up on the X rays of my mother's liver. She calls the spot a "development," as if it is something promising, like a housing project. Her hands move quickly as she talks. The backs of them are tanned from her work in the garden. The palms, flashing white as she speaks, remind me of the undersides of maple leaves exposed in a wind. With her hands my mother can make small houses, a street intersection, a car going out of control.

"Well, it just went poof," she said once, explaining to my father and grandmother where the grocery money had gone and why we were having hot dogs once again for our Sunday dinner. "Like that," she said, and her hands described baroque scrolls of smoke above her dinner plate. It seemed to me that with her hands she might produce, out of the imaginary smoke, an emerald bird, inside of which would be a golden egg, inside of which would be a lifetime supply of grocery money.

My father, ever mindful of my education, cast a meaningful eye my way and said, "Although a hot dog on a bun is not the feast we had all hoped for this afternoon, let us remember that it contains more protein than the average Chinese person eats in a week."

"I am not a Chinese," my grandmother said, looking sideways at my mother. "I am a Protestant."

"I'll need time to think about this new development," my mother says now. "I'll need time to plan." My father has been dead for five years, and my grandmother three. Not long before he died, my father moved the family, without consulting anyone, from a large house on the edge of town to a smaller one near the center. He was thinking ahead to their old age, he told me. The smaller house was near drugstores and super-markets, and closer to the hardware store he ran. It was near the hospital in case of emergency. The Christmas after he bought the house, he drove me into the country-side to discuss the future.

"These are the insurance policies, this is the will." He handed me thick brown envelopes. "This is the key to the safe-deposit box. Do not let your mother sell that house when I am gone. It is in a good location for old people." I had been home from college only two days, but already I felt like a child again, inarticulate and fearful. I felt the old speech rhythms return, the trun-cated syntax, the vague euphemistic vocabulary, and a sense that there were always secrets to be kept from someone else in the family.

"You're still alive," I said. We walked down a slope to a pond, sliding on the crusted snow.

"I've arranged it so that your mother will not be able to get her hands on all of the money at once," he said.

I thought of her back at the house, wrapping presents with my grandmother. I thought of how pleased she had looked as my father and I left the house, suspecting, perhaps, that we were going to collect a surprise Christmas present. Instead, we stood at the edge of the pond as the sun went down, and defined the limits of her future—where she could live, how much she could spend, who would die first—as if her life were a geometric pattern, something that could be drawn with ruled sides and with perfect arcs spun off the tip of a compass.

The sun slid behind a row of fir trees, and the pond glowed lavender near the shadows of the opposite bank. "The ice is too thick this winter," my father said. "There's no light at the bottom of this pond. The water plants will die and then the fish will die, too." He spoke matter-of-factly. It was not his pond. "If we don't have a thaw, the farmer will have to come out here and drill holes to save the fish." He paused and looked at me. He seemed about to suggest a lesson in life. "It's a good thing we do not live in the country," he said. "Your mother and grandmother think they would like to live in the country, but it is better for them to live in town."

The following summer, he died. Two winters later, my grandmother died, not long after falling on the ice in front of our house. There was a step she had forgotten about, at the juncture of our walk and the city sidewalk.

It was not a badly designed step—just one that, in her old age, she had overlooked.

Aunt Ruda knows that something is up. Every day for the last two weeks, my mother has been going through closets and trunks and throwing away things that once belonged to my father and grandmother. Old shoes, shirts, dresses, sweaters, cheap jewelry, soured cologne still in its Christmas box, gun magazines, clippings of inspirational pieces from Christian newsletters. Ruda stands on the porch and frowns at the seven garbage bags sitting by the curb.

"She's selling the house, isn't she?" Ruda says. My father was Ruda's brother, and now she takes a proprietary interest in the house on his behalf. "If she moves into the country, she'll never be able to get out of her drive in winter."

"I don't know what she's doing," I say truthfully.

In a spiral notebook, I have made an orderly list of the decisions that must soon be made about my mother's chemotherapy treatments. Where will she have them—in California with me, or in Ohio, near Ruda and the other relatives? Should a registered nurse be engaged? Should a housekeeper be brought in? My mother ignores the notebook and moves through the house in a distracted way, bumping into furniture. "This house is too small," she tells me. "It was designed for short people." She has decided to remodel the kitchen, and she presses me for advice. "Do you like harvest yellow or that green color?"

"I don't know." I am impatient with her, anxious to deal with the crisis at hand. She pretends that this is like any other summer, that once, a year ago, she was sick and gaunt but now she is well again. It is early July and the serious heat is here, moist and languid, settling upon the town like sleep. In the evenings we drive into the cooler countryside in search of air-conditioned rural restaurants. My mother eats hearty meals—mashed potatoes and gravy, fried chicken, buttered corn. I think about her liver struggling to sort out the proteins, the fats, the poisons. Something must be done. She lingers over the menu, wondering whether to order liver and bacon, liver and onions, or chicken livers in wine and sour cream. Watching her, I wonder whether this is an unwitting irony or part of a secret plan to attack the diseased cells with surrogates. Suddenly I can imagine them, the bad cells, as cartoon cousins to my evil kidney, planning their defense with small knives and guns and miniature cannons.

Under her bed I find a stack of new books, optimistic in their clean dust jackets. *Mind Over Matter. Long Life and Nutrition.* In the mornings, when she thinks I am reading the newspaper on the porch, she goes into the kitchen and blends a viscous concoction of raw eggs, goat's milk, brewer's yeast, honey, kelp, bananas, wheat germ, cooked rice—everything she has ever heard was good for one's health. I am a spy in the house. In her desk I find a brochure describing a health spa in Mexico where inoperable patients are given a vegetable diet and coffee enemas. In her purse I find a newspaper clipping about a Catholic shrine in Indiana, where blind people are able to see again and arthritics stand up straight. Her disease is becoming a secret that each of us keeps from the other. At night, after she has gone to bed, I read about the side effects of chemotherapy. I discover that one of the chemicals used in what is called "chemotherapy" is similar to the fuels used in jet airplanes.

"Rachel has a secret," my grandmother said to my father at the dinner table that Sunday as they sat before their hot dogs and wondered why the grocery budget, so carefully calculated by my father, was so badly mismanaged by my mother. It was true. My mother did have a secret. Since her marriage, she had never had a job, and now she had decided to go to work. She had decided to become an American Fragrance Lady, selling cosmetics and perfumes door to door. For weeks she had been taking a few dollars from the various household budgets in order to raise the capital for the initial investment. She invited me along the day she went to collect the merchandise from the regional representative. I was fourteen years old and already beginning to talk in the superior way my grandmother and father had, but still she took me into her confidence. On my lap I held the huge envelope of fugitive dollar bills.

"Maybe I'll let you take a few of the products around to some of the high-school girls," she said, already imagining the empire we would build, a magical place where money flew out of every house and followed us through the streets.

"She always had secrets when she was a kid," my grandmother continued. "She used to steal money from my purse."

"That was me," I said. "I stole quarters." It was a joke, a diversionary tactic. My mother smiled faintly.

"You stole from your grandmother?" my father said.

"So did Rachel," my grandmother said. "This is a wonderful family."

"Oh, for heaven's sake," said my mother. She left

the room and returned carrying the American Fragrance display case, which she placed on the table and snapped open to reveal the rows of glittering bottles. They were made of heavy glass in red, blue, and opaque white, and were cast in the shapes of the Liberty Bell, Independence Hall, and other national monuments. I think there was a moment, as she lifted a red bottle in the shape of the Lincoln Memorial and held it to the light of the window so that it sparkled like a gemstone, when she actually thought my father might be pleased by the prospect of his wife going from door to door, to his friends and his neighbors and his customers at the hardware store.

Without looking at her, he picked up the mustard knife and said, "If you have a private matter to discuss with me, we will discuss it after dinner."

I didn't hear the conversation. I imagine it was brief and sensible. My father would have been organized and logical, using the legal tablet to calculate the triviality of her projected profits. He would have reminded her that she did not have, after all, the aggressive personality of a saleslady. Perhaps he made fun of the products, their ludicrous shapes, their dubious smells. Perhaps he simply said no. I never saw the display case again. My mother never set out into the neighborhood dressed in a suit and the heavily applied makeup prescribed by the American Fragrance regional representative.

"I don't have fifteen hundred dollars a week," my mother is saying. She says it so sharply that it sounds like an accusation. "Do you have fifteen hundred dollars a week?" I am young and healthy. I grew up in a family of three adults. Tap lessons, ballet, clarinet, piano, western-saddle riding lessons, English-saddle, a college education, graduate school, a job in California. I am the one who escaped this house.

All morning she has sat on this porch and torn photographs out of old albums, ripped them into halves, and thrown them in a garbage bag by her feet. I awoke earlier than I usually do, and when I came downstairs I saw her there, through the gauze of the living-room curtains, seated near the trellis of honeysuckle vines. I watched as she held the pictures before she tore them up. They trembled in her hands like caught animals. It seemed to me that she was destroying my own past, pictures of herself with me, my father, my grandmother, my brother. Something must be done. I decided to force the issue. I went out to the porch and asked where—exactly where and how—she would like to begin treatment for the spot on her liver, which was not a development but cancer. She put the albums aside and closed the garbage bag with a twist tie. She gave me a long, stern look, as if I were an adversary, and said, "Switzerland."

Switzerland? What was in Switzerland?

"A place where they give you mineral baths and chemicals that don't make you sicker than you already are."

"All right," I said. A place in Switzerland was better than no place at all. "Let's look into it."

She already had. The place in Switzerland would cost fifteen hundred dollars a week, plus air fare. Our medical insurance would cover most of the treatment if the clinic were in America, but it was not. I thought of the American Fragrance venture and wondered whether she was thinking of it, too—of how the sale of a thousand little Plymouth Rocks and Empire State Buildings might have bought her, if not health, then at least the rarefied air and the beguiling sunlight on the side of an Alpine mountain.

"Do you have fifteen hundred dollars a week?" she says again.

"Fifteen hundred dollars for a mineral bath?" I say it too quickly, too callously, my own hysteria turning to flippancy. "Can't you find a mineral bath in America?"

She stands up. Her hands are fists. "I don't want to lose my hair," she says. She walks past me to the other end of the porch and says it again. "I don't want to lose my hair. Do you want your own mother to lose her hair?" And now suddenly the stiffness leaves her body, the accusation melts in the summer heat. She returns to the far end of the porch and studies the honeysuckle vines that she planted six years ago, when my father bought the house. She reaches up and begins to unwind a runner that spirals toward the ceiling of the porch. "If you let them grow straight up, they'll just droop from the roof and look sloppy," she says. She begins to rewind it along a horizontal piece of lath. Her fingers are so long and supple in the green light that she seems to be winding her own hands into the latticework. "I'm going to phone your Aunt Ruda for some advice," she says at last. "She knows all about doctors and diseases."

While she is on the phone, I hurry through the photo albums and the garbage bag to see what can be salvaged. Here is a picture of my mother and father, looking younger than I am now, at the seashore. Here is one of the five of us in our best clothes in front of my father's hardware store. I want to weep. I see that my mother's target has not been the family, as I had imagined. It has been merely the pictures of herself that are blurry or unflattering. All morning she has labored on the family photo albums like an editor, expurgating the ugly likenesses of herself in order to leave an attractive vision for me when she is gone.

My mother went to bed early this evening. She sleeps ten hours a day now, taking care of herself. I watched television until two in the morning. On a talk show there was a woman who researches death. She has made a living by talking to people who are dying or who have nearly died. She has asked them what the approach of death is like. She told the talk-show host that what she learned should make everyone hopeful and happy. "We never die alone," she said. In all the case histories she studied, the dying people reported that they were with a loved one who had preceded them in death. The heart-attack victims in surgery, the drowning victims called back from death by mouth-to-mouth resuscitation, the badly mutilated victims of automobile accidents, the weak and frail and palsied in their hospital beds—all of them, she said, reported that they were in the presence of loved ones who came through the dark to be at their sides. The woman was a doctor, middle-aged and passionate. She spoke with a German accent, surely the voice of science. I moved closer to the television and listened carefully, wanting to believe her.

Now the screen is foggy blue, and I can hear the deep sighs of my mother's sleep float in the stairwell. I think of how at nine o'clock she rose from the chintz-covered chair and went up the stairs with a fierce, eager step, the hem of her white robe rippling behind in a satin fury, like water swooshing uphill. "Don't forget the lights," she said. "Electricity costs money." And that simple injunction, which I have heard all my life, smoothed out the fabric of our terrible day. Don't forget the lights, don't let the screen door slam, don't tramp snow across the carpet—this is the language that circumscribes domestic life, making it compact and manageable. I snap off the television and turn off the lights—this one between the chintz-covered chairs, this one by the sofa, and this one on top of the newel post—grateful for the small instruction that tells how to end the day. If my mother could choose the loved ones who would meet her at death's threshold, I wonder whether she would choose my father and grandmother, the people who established the narrow pattern of her life and handed down the judgments.

...

It's come to this—a linen-covered table, shrimp salads in a country club. Ruda brought us here to meet the "medical counselor," a youngish woman who wears a silk dress and heavy jewelry. I can see that she makes my mother feel awkward, almost obsequious, yet cautiously hopeful. My mother handles her silverware with too much care, as if the knife and fork had razor tips. On the way here, Ruda cheered us up with cancer success stories. There was one about a man who laughed himself into good health while he was locked in a hotel room with a movie screen and prints of all the Three Stooges films.

"Is this woman a psychiatrist?" I asked. "Is she an M.D.?"

"She's a professional," Ruda said. "She studied at an institute." Ruda says she does not feel well herself. She has high blood pressure, and heart attacks run in the family, she reminds us.

"I always like to have the family here on the first session," the counselor says. She puts a hand on Ruda's arm and a hand on mine. "I want you to close your eyes and think of this image. It came to me in a dream last night when I knew I was going to meet you." Her voice is like Muzak—an uninspired hum, too sweet. Ruda closes her eyes and bows her head, as if in prayer. My mother looks at me quickly. She did not expect dream therapy.

"The image is a bowl of pink crystals. Can you see them? Translucent and pure. I want you both to imagine that you are eating these crystals every day. I want you to say to yourselves, 'I am eating the wholeness of crystals, and they are faith, hope, and responsibility.' "

My mother looks at me again, anxiously. Ruda's eyes are still closed; so are the counselor's.

"I have trouble picturing a bowl of pink crystals," my mother says.

I remove my arm from the counselor's hand. "How about a bowl of chocolate buttercreams?" I say.

My mother says to the counselor, "I know my daughter and Ruda already have faith, hope, and responsibility. They don't have to pretend."

When I was about six, I nearly died of a kidney infection. It was very cold outside, perhaps twenty degrees below zero. On the inside corner of my bedroom window a frond of ice bloomed and unfurled across the glass. I was feverish, my face felt like burning paper. I got out of bed and laid my cheek against the ice. My mother took me to the hospital in an ambulance. It was night and we were alone. My father was in another state on temporary duty, and my grandmother had not come to live with us yet. My mother carried me out to the ambulance herself and sang a little song as someone placed ice packs around my body. She sang the little tune, and made up words in her soft, airy voice as she went along. "We're going on a little trip, we're not afraid of the night." It was cold in the ambulance. She leaned over me as she sang, and put her hand on my forehead. I could see her breath misting white in the darkness and it seemed to me that she was exhaling light.

The weather has been peculiar this summer—first the clear days in June and now a fog in early August, as a cold front sweeps across the state and the warm ground sends a mist into the air. It is after midnight, and my mother and I are walking arm in arm along the sidewalk under the maple trees. A while ago, she got out of bed and came downstairs to find me in front of the television. "You can't sleep, either, can you?" she said. "Neither can I." She made us cups of hot cocoa, as if I were the young child again, and she the young mother. "You'd think we could sleep now that it is cooler," she said.

I watch her breath as we walk—white puffs of light that seem to phosphorize the air around us.

"Actually, what I'd like to do sometime is go to Japan and have a meal at one of those places where you get the soup with the fish eggs," she is saying. "Or maybe to China, where they bring the soup to the table with the chicken feet still in it."

I nod. It is not too late to sell the house. We could fly around the world. We could eat grape leaves in Greece. We could eat camel ankles in Ethiopia. "They're very frugal, those people," I say. "They can make anything tasty." I imagine the two of us seated serenely before a small meal in a house in the Himalayas, where the Hunzas, who live to a hundred but have no term for old age, feast on apricot blossoms in the spring.

"Your grandmother never liked foreigners. They weren't Christian enough for her, but I've always thought they were probably as happy as we are."

The word *happy* surprises me. All summer I have regarded us as miserable. My mother stops under a halo of light. The fog hangs among the trees like veils of trailing lace. She smiles. "Well, if it's going to be this cold in the summer, I just wish for your sake we could be cold someplace fun, like Bavaria." She pulls the sweater together in front of her breasts and hugs herself. It is late and she is tired. We have walked too far.

I reach out to touch her, to offer the support of my arm around her shoulders, and she leans easily against my body, as if I were the mother, strong, cheerful, controlling a small bubble of space in which there is no time, only light and warmth. I recall the German woman doctor on television, earnest and importunate, making the plea for faith: We never die alone. A car skids on rain-slick pavement, an airplane dives into the sea, a hospital bed defines at last the perimeter of a mortal life—yet we are never alone. Embracing my mother, I embrace belief itself. Suddenly, I want us to be back at the house, rooting through the refrigerator for leftover chicken and sweet tomatoes—a midwestern feast.

"It's all right," I say to my mother, holding her close in the fog. "Everything will be all right."

*S*uddenly the world is composed of infinitely divisible parts, and things, it seems, grow bigger as they grow smaller. An atom, once a tiny creature, is now a giant compared to a quark. And inside the quark, who knows? Maybe a whole universe of colliding specks, some of them red-haired, some blond, some sleek and dusky skinned, some of them with silicone implants, and some of the plainer ones, like me, still going to the shopping center in thrift-shop shoes.

Harvey has a former wife named Susu, and who am I? A single woman and not getting any younger: I can settle for a compromise.

Harvey's former wife has given us both lice, serially, of course, first to Harvey, who passed them right along to me. For the two years since the divorce she's been living in Italy, where she uses the money from the sale of their house to finance the reinvention of her face and figure—a thinner nose and bigger breasts. Also

thicker eyelashes—three hundred dollars per trans-
plant from an unspecified part of her body. For two
weeks now, she has been sleeping on Harvey's sofa, but,
you know, as my friend Lila likes to say, people who did
it once can do it again, and anyway with husbands and
wives there's always the long good-bye. "Smile," Lila
says. "Keep your sense of humor. Everything will be all
right."

"She was my wife," Harvey says, as we drive
around the shopping center looking for a space near the
self-serve drugstore. "I was married to her," he says,
enunciating the word *married* as if it were part of a
foreign language I have not yet mastered.

"It's certainly a comfort to know these are just
postconnubial crabs," I say, and Harvey laughs.

He stops the car in a loading zone and hunches
over the wheel like a getaway driver. When I push
through the plate-glass door I look back and see him
glancing over his shoulder for signs of people who will
recognize us and, with their extrasensory perception,
discern immediately that we are on a shady errand. At
the rear of the store I find what I am looking for, a
selection of colorful boxes advertising a cure for certain
skin conditions and, in smaller print, for three different
kinds of lice infestation. These boxes are prominently

displayed next to an arrangement of condoms and sper-
micidal jellies, and free pamphlets describing sexually
transmitted diseases. Next to them is a line of eight
people, most of them well-groomed older women waiting
for their prescriptions. I decide to linger near cough
remedies and hemorrhoid preparations, but now here
come two more people to the prescription line.

"Take me to the Women's Health Collective," I
tell Harvey back in the car. "We need the privacy of a
prescription."

"You know you can get these things off of toilets
now," he says. "You can even get them off of sofas and
chairs in even very clean houses."

"We know where we got these, Harvey."

"Okay, you take the wheel, and I'll go in."

Now it's my turn to drive around the shopping
center, through the clots of Saturday morning traffic and
fearful pedestrians. This is the very place where Harvey
and I met just nine months ago only moments after I hit
his parked car, and now here we are raising a family of
tiny creatures.

"I was daydreaming," I said. "I didn't think to
look before I made my cut."

"It's my fault," he said. "I parked too close." It
was his voice that attracted me to him first, rich and

golden like oak turned to sound, a big, solid voice a person could lean against. Then there was his height, six feet four inches of him; even now I think there must be enough of Harvey to go around, while there is so little of me that when I offer affection to someone, I feel as if I am handing over some of my very cells. Harvey loves everyone, and I love only Harvey.

"I don't know much about small cars," I told him. I was driving the enormous old Ford I had had since college. "Is yours a Datsun or a Toyota?"

"It's an Audi," he said, and then he added, before I had the time to become depressed by the prospect of increased insurance premiums, "Don't worry. I'm very handy. I think I can knock out that dent with a hammer."

Now he stands by the curb in front of the drugstore, a huge man with a very small sack in his hand. "I hope you got enough for three," I say. "Well," he says, "I ran into someone from the office. I had to buy this instead." Inside the sack is a bottle of dandruff shampoo.

"Why can't we get Susu to do this?" I say as we enter the freeway traffic on our way to the Women's Health Collective, which is twelve miles from here and suitably anonymous. I love to say the name "Susu." I say it so that the name sounds ridiculous, and it helps me to think of Susu as a ridiculous person instead of a lovesick woman just like me. Every morning for two weeks Susu has been going into the bathroom with ordinary, sleep-flattened hair and emerging an hour later with a rococo tangle of back-combed frizzes and knotted tendrils. "Her hair looks like a place where small animals go to browse in the night," I say to Harvey. "But what am I saying? Her hair *is* a place where small animals go to browse in the night."

"She's always on the verge of a nervous collapse," Harvey says.

This much I know about the marriage. Susu took many weight-reducing pills and cried a great deal, while Harvey was complimentary and apologetic. When Susu was angry, she threw plates. When Harvey was angry, he went to his office and spent the night designing small houses that will never be built—modular units for the common people, each unit embellished with a medieval detail. "But who wants lancet windows when they can have a second bathroom instead?" Harvey likes to say, making the houses sound like a fool's invention. But the houses—and there are dozens of them now—are his secret hopes, the places where he can curl up in his mind's eye when times get bad.

"Look," Harvey says. "It's not like this is AIDS or anything. It's not even herpes. It's not even a urinary tract infection."

My friend Lila is an engineer who would like to be an antiques dealer or maybe the curator of a small museum. "I think I missed my century," she likes to say. "I think I would have been very happy doing needlepoint pictures in 1750."

Instead Lila has worked for ten years in the semiconductor industry developing new ways to make a computer smaller than your hand. "In 1750 you would have been a washerwoman," I tell her. "Or maybe a slave." Lila is an adopted child. She has dark skin and light gray eyes. She could be anybody, a Scandinavian Indian or an Irish black woman. She grew up in a series of mobile-home parks and now lives in an apartment full of authentic Chippendale and Hepplewhite, baroque silver, and antique beaded purses.

"Be sure and ask for Dr. L'Heureux," she tells me now as I stand at a pay phone across the street from the Women's Health Collective. "Dr. L'Heureux is the one who will be lighthearted and make you feel that the situation is very funny."

As it turns out, Dr. L'Heureux is on vacation in

Hawaii, and the young receptionist at the desk does not think that anyone is available right now. You would think that a place called the Women's Health Collective would be staffed with sympathetic, generous-hearted people. But except for the absence of men, this place is like any other large clinic, with people on the front desk who make you feel that dealing with your medical problem is an inconvenience.

"This is a gynecological problem?" the receptionist says very loudly. "Yes," I say in a low voice meant to be a cue.

"And you can't come back and see us on Monday?"

"No," I say, trying to give the word just the right degree of quiet urgency.

She consults once again the form I have just filled out. "You have an infection?"

"No, that word is infestation."

"You have a yeast infection?"

"No, I don't." I am thirty-one years old and have never had a yeast infection or cystitis. I also never have had gonorrhea, syphilis, or an abortion. I have a checkup once a year and am a healthy specimen. I bend close to the small curve of the woman's ear and say, "I have"—and here my voice drops away altogether as I feel the loathsome word scraping along the back of my throat—"I have the crubs."

"CRUBS? You have CRUBS?" She is perplexed, then amused. She smiles, unsure whether I have intentionally made a joke or am one of those patients the medical people like to laugh about on their coffee breaks—uneducated women who cannot name their parts and say "bajiva" instead of "vagina," or rich women who say they got the clap from the cleaning woman who brought germs to the bathroom. "I have the crubs," I say again, this time as loudly as the receptionist, because now everyone in the waiting room has already heard it anyway, and the doctors will be told, and the nurse practitioners, and the med techs and the janitors. Suddenly I can imagine the lice down there building a new life for themselves in the wilderness of my pubic hair, clearing the forests, planting farms, and sending east for a spinster schoolteacher. "I have the crubs," I say. "And I need help now."

"Well, at least you know nobody's going to have any sex for the next few days," Lila says. We are resting at the edge of the apartment pool between our laps. I admire Lila's slender, muscular legs and think that Susu would pay ten thousand dollars for those legs if the surgeons

in Italy could figure out a way to make them. It is early
evening, the water is cool, the oleanders are still in
bloom, there is a fragrance of invisible eucalyptus trees
in the air, and behind the apartment building, the red
sunlight billows like sheet silk. This is not a bad life.

"My first husband's ex-wife was just like her," Lila
says. "She had lots of affairs but always went back to
him in between to be told that she was still a desirable
woman."

"You think this could go on indefinitely?" I have
a vision of Harvey and me seated at a candlelit table
twenty years from now in one of his small Gothic
houses, and in from the kitchen comes Susu with her
large Italian breasts and a nose that is beginning to slide
out of place like an old boxer's.

"Maybe she'll marry a plastic surgeon," Lila says.

We look up toward Harvey's lighted kitchen window, where Susu is preparing supper. Harvey is bent
over the dining table like a willow tree, while Susu
stands by the counter like a box hedge. "I think the time
has come for me to have a little talk with the happy
couple," I say.

Susu's meal for the three of us consists of a packaged
spaghetti dinner and, on the side, some slices of canned

pineapple decorating small bowls of cottage cheese. "Look what Susu did," Harvey says, giving me a cautious glance.

"How nice, Susu. Did you learn this in Italy?"

Susu laughs as we sit down at the table. That is one good thing about her: she can usually take a joke.

"Susu was always a rotten cook, wasn't I, sweetie?" Susu says to Harvey. Why does she have that coy way of referring to herself in the third person, as if she's a character even in her own life?

"Really, this is great," Harvey says. I see that he has decided to discuss this meal at length in order to avoid more delicate topics. "Would you believe that she did all this in only twenty minutes?"

Already he is halfway through his meal, and I realize once again that this is a Harvey I have not seen much of in the nine months since I dented the side of his car. This is a Harvey who is attracted to food largely because it is fuel, and whose heart is gladdened as much by the sight of the kind that comes pulpy from a can as by my own aromatic sauce, simmered for hours with fresh herbs. In the last two weeks I have discovered that Harvey really cannot tell the difference between scrambled eggs and a soufflé or between Campbell's chicken noodle soup and the kind I make from scratch.

"No wonder you're so thin," Susu says to me. "You're not eating anything."

"Maybe I need some silicone implants," I say, and I am just mean and small enough to feel a thrill of pleasure when Susu looks back at her plate without smiling. Harvey gives me a warning look. Susu, I must remember, is not playing with a full deck this week. Apparently, this is her best culinary effort, and it has been offered as a peace token—Susu, the repentant crab-carrier trying to make amends with the other woman.

"I was never pretty," she says. "I always had these big hips and no breasts to go with them. Not like you, Angelina. You have a nice compact little figure."

"Yes, you do," Harvey says to me. "And you have one, too. Both of your figures have always been very nice."

"You always lie," Susu says. "You lie to make everybody feel good about you."

That is not true. In fact, Harvey never lies. He is simply one of those people who rarely perceive an inadequacy in another person. Right now I can see the old guilt resurrecting itself as I watch Harvey watching Susu over a shaker of Kraft cheese and a plate of soft white bread. He is about to take the blame once again for the failure of the marriage. I can see the tenderness in his eyes, the pity that will cause him to offer Susu a place to stay for weeks and weeks if that's how long it takes her to find a job. She begins to cry, and Harvey reaches out to touch her hand.

"Now come on," he says in his beautiful voice.

"Excuse me," I say, although no one is listening. I leave the apartment and go back over to Lila's.

"He was always a sucker for the basket cases," she says. "After her he went out with a sculptress who had had shock treatment and who used to send him obscene, jealous postcards at the office. Then he took up with a woman who ate only fruit and nuts and liked to throw drinks on other women at parties."

"Don't you ever want to get married again?" I say. "Don't you want to move into a little house with daffodils pushing up along the front walk in the spring?"

"Listen, I have thousands of dollars' worth of antiques and a good job. Things could be worse. I could be in love with a man like Harvey."

Every Sunday night Harvey and I watch the science program on the PBS channel. Tonight we are watching it on Harvey's bed with the door closed and the volume turned up high, so that we cannot be overheard by Susu, who is pretending to read foreign-language fashion magazines in the next room.

"She's actually a sweet person," he says. "She's having a hard time thinking about her future."

"How can she think with a hairdo like that? Her brain never gets any light or air."

"Please," he says. "Please, please, please."

Last week's topic on the PBS program was atoms and quarks. This week the program is about the miracles of microphotography. Harvey and I watch with genuine fascination as a lens focuses on a human eyelid and magnifies it fifty thousand times to reveal that there are tiny, fish-shaped mites living between the hairs. The announcer says that these mites live on everyone.

"See," says Harvey. "We already had things living on our bodies."

In the next scene, the amazing lens focuses on a piece of ordinary bedroom carpet to reveal that in between the fibers there are thousands of living dust mites, each much smaller than the head of a pin. These dust mites, the announcer explains, are in all our homes. They subsist entirely on the cells of sloughed-off human skin. Harvey gets down on the floor and crawls around the bed on his hands and knees. He rests his chin on the sheets by my foot. "Skin," he murmurs and kisses my little toe.

"We can't do anything before Monday or Tuesday," I say, really just as a test of how much he wants me. "We all have to give our bodies another chemical shampoo before we're safe."

He moves his head along my leg and kisses the inside of my thigh. "We can fool around," he says.

"Hello, hello," a voice says from the other side of the door. "Anybody alive in there? *Les personae morte?*"

"What language is it speaking?" I say.

Harvey crawls to the door and opens it a crack. "I can't find the detergent," Susu says to me. "What's the matter with him?"

"Harvey is a dust mite."

"He was always like this, you know. So neat you could never find even the most common thing."

"Back in a second," Harvey says as he stands up and steps into the hall. I notice that he shrewdly leaves the door open so that I can monitor the search for the soap. But Susu drops the subject of detergent as soon as they reach the kitchen and begins to tell another one of her third-person stories about life in Italy. In this one Susu goes riding on the beach on the Riviera although she has never been on a horse before. "So there goes

Susu in her bikini and there goes Greggie galloping ahead of me." I wonder whether Greggie is the one with the insect problem. On television the dust mites stand like tiny armadillos among colossal strands of shag carpet. In the kitchen Susu's horse kneels toward the beach because he wants to take a sand bath. " 'Mi scuzi, ' I say to the Italians. I think the horse is dying. 'Help, help!' " In this anecdote, Susu is the silly, helpless person who needs to be protected. I hear Harvey's deep laugh, and I close the door and turn off the television. I get in bed as I hear Susu say, "Yes, I did, I did." I put the pillow over my head. "I did. It was unbelievable."

I stretch over Harvey's part of the bed and think of the dust mites alive all over the room. There must be whole families of them, generations and generations, living off the great god Harvey as his cells float through the air like manna. Probably after these last nine months a few colonies of Angelinites have sprung up, too. I wonder whether different species have grown dependent on different tastes—cells flavored by spaghetti sauce, or spilled alcohol, or chocolate syrup, perfumed cells from breasts and inner thighs—Chanel No. 5, L'Air du Temps, Heaven Scent—creamed cells from hands and faces, cells lathered thick with lipstick (these would be Susu's cells), and maybe right now a whole

SWEET TALK · 94

race of dust mites is dividing itself into small communities and setting out in covered wagons for more fertile shag, and the community that has been subsisting on Pond's Dry Skin Cream begins to die out when I switch, arbitrarily, to another brand. I can imagine the dust-mite priests down there pleading for cells saturated with lanolin, cornstarch, rosewater, building little fires, chanting beads, trying to make do with Oil of Olay cells, to which they are allergic.

"Andiamo," says Susu as I gallop toward sleep.

It is 7 A.M. on Monday morning, and Susu's underwear blooms around the bathroom like California poppies. There are scarlet-orange bras hanging from the towel racks, each bra cup stitched in concentric circles meant to suggest a target. There are scarlet-orange panties— some with cut-out crotches—dripping their color along the plastic of the shower curtain. And in the tub and sink there is more underwear seeping mauve into the sudsy water.

"Where are the whips, Harvey?" I say when he comes to stand behind me in the doorway. "Where are the chains?"

He laughs. "I thought she was doing this stuff last night."

"This does not look to me like the underwear of Emily Dickinson," I say.

"Shh," he says, still laughing. "She'll hear you."

"For God's sake, it's seven o'clock in the morning," I say loudly. "Please tell Miss Frederick's of Hollywood we would like to take a shower."

"Here is Miss Frederick's in person," Susu says, stepping between us into the bathroom. "Please excuse Miss Frederick's if she has to wash the lice out of her clothes before she goes to her job interview."

"Everybody's been excusing you for two weeks," I say. "When are you leaving?"

"Maybe we could all go into the kitchen and have some coffee," Harvey says.

"I gave you the only three thin years I ever had in my life," Susu says to Harvey. "And what did you give me in return? You gave me lice."

I look at Harvey. "You had lice when you were married?" Harvey looks away.

"He gave me lice last week," Susu says and sits on the edge of the tub.

"He couldn't have given you lice," I say. "He gave them to me." But somewhere in the back of my head a camera lens is panning the landscape of my life, and a tree is no longer a tree but a place where other lives and whole worlds will be revealed if the eye looks closely enough at what's under the bark.

Susu begins to cry. "I had to put up with this for years," she says. "You think you're so special? You think you're the only signorina on the block?"

"I suppose now we're going to have to hear a story about the virgin birth of the crabs," I say. I feel that all my good qualities—restraint, perceptiveness, and the ability to handle bad luck—are being stripped away in a violent wind, and I am trying to hold everything together with a joke. I look toward Harvey, but he has slipped into another room. I sit on the edge of the tub and lean against the wet shower curtain. "It was my pal Lila," I say. "Wasn't it?"

Here is what I do at work: I make small houses, office buildings, even airports. I also make streets, trees, shrubs, flower beds, ponds, streams, and miniature people. I work for a large group of architects, creating three-dimensional mock-ups of their designs. Harvey still talks about leaving the firm and going into business for himself. Lila is thinking about going back to graduate school in art history. Susu sells real estate but would rather have a job in broadcasting. I am the only person I know happy at work, except for a writer I met the other night at a party. He has pale green eyes and hair so thick it makes me think his brain must be a very fertile place. His name is Anthony, which is the name of the patron of lost things. An irony, since he owns so few of the things the rest of us seem to regard as necessities. He lives in a one-room apartment furnished in someone else's taste.

"I think he lives in his head," I tell Lila. "I think in his head he owns stereo sets and three-piece suits and takes trips to Mexico in the winter." Lila and I are sitting on one of her Persian carpets near a cherry cabinet full of beaded antique purses. It's been two months since I stopped seeing Harvey, and now Lila and I are having drinks to demonstrate that we are still friends, as indeed we are. If I could choose to be someone else I might actually choose to be Lila, who is smart and beautiful, and whom everybody likes, but who seems to have found a way to close the door of this museum of an apartment and ignore the mucky terrain over which the rest of us must walk. For me the closed door is my work, where I create a stationary world, ageless and colorful, a shopping center or school no bigger than the top of a desk, and completely manageable.

"Once a week he comes over here to tell me how

much he misses you," Lila says. She is talking about Harvey. I truly am not interested, so I turn and open the cabinet to look at the purses. Each purse is covered with glass beads and, I see, each bead is faceted so that it gives off many pinpoints of light. "He thinks that you're perfect," Lila says. "He thinks you're a nice cross between Susu, who is crazy, and me. I'm much too independent for just about everybody." We have already established that in Harvey's life Lila occurred briefly between the sculptress and the fruit-and-nut woman, and that she reentered it briefly during the Susu-and-me period. I truly do not care, I told her. I now look back on those months as a phase of temporary insanity that began with an accident in a parking lot.

"You can tell Harvey that I do not wish to be attractive to someone because of my characteristics as a hybrid."

"You're crazy, too," Lila says. "You're a dreamer, you don't have any courage."

"I'm not unhappy," I say. "I'm fine." All week long I have been working on the Janet Freeman Elementary School project, which may be the last elementary school built in California for a generation, now that the taxpayers have voted once again against education. This school will slide on Teflon joints during the earthquakes and will save all the children and the teachers. "Besides, I've just met this writer. He only owns seven shirts and doesn't have any other girlfriends. He leads a simple life." Already I can imagine the two of us moving to the country. Lila leaves the room to refill the drinks, and I turn back to the purses, where there are beads giving off light of every color, amethyst light and rose light, gold and platinum light, the silver light of oat fields in early summer, the coppery light of rivers stirring with mud after a spring thaw. Each bead twinkles like an eye, and it seems to me that if you could get close enough to one it would be like looking into a pupil to see your own reflection, and in the background there would be trees and hills and bridges, each bead different, here a mountainscape in the Himalayas, tiny goats grazing below the snow line, there a tropical shore in Rarotonga, pink orchids strewn across the sand, and always in the foreground, the oval face of Angelina.

I grew up in the Army. About the only kind of dove I ever saw was a dead dove resting small-boned upon a dinner plate. Even though we were Protestants and Bible readers, no one regarded the dove sentimentally as a symbol of peace—the bird who had flown back to Noah carrying the olive branch, as if to say, "The land is green again, come back to the land." When I was thirteen, my family moved to Fort Sill, Oklahoma, only a few weeks before the dove-hunting season opened. My father, who liked to tinker with guns on weekends, sat down at the dining-room table one Saturday and unwrapped a metal device called the Lombreglia Self-Loader. The Self-Loader was a crimping mechanism that enabled a person to assemble shotgun ammunition at home. "Save Money and Earn Pleasure," the box label said. "For the Self-Reliant Sportsman Who Wants to Do the Job Right!"

"If you can learn to handle this," my father said, "you can load my shells for me when the hunting season arrives." He was addressing my brother, MacArthur, who was ten years old. We pulled up chairs to the table, while my mother and grandmother remained near the light of the kitchen door. My father delivered a little lecture on the percussive action of the firing pin as he set out the rest of the loading equipment—empty red cartridges, cardboard wads, brass caps, a bowl of gunpowder, and several bowls of lead shot. He spoke in his officer's briefing-room voice—a voice that seemed to say, "This will be a difficult mission, soldier, but I know you are up to the mark." MacArthur seemed to grow taller listening to that voice, his spine perfectly erect as he helped align the equipment in the center of the table. My father finished the lecture by explaining that the smallest-size shot was best for dove or quail, the medium size was best for duck or rabbit, and the largest size was best for goose or wild turkey.

"And which size shot is best for humans?" my grandmother said. She did not disapprove of guns, but she could rarely pass up a chance to say something sharp to my father. My grandmother was a member of the WCTU, and he was conducting this lesson in between sips of a scotch-and-soda.

"It depends," my father said. "It depends on whether you want to eat the person afterward."

"Well, ha, ha," my grandmother said.

"It is a lot of work trying to prize small shot out of a large body," my father said.

"Very funny," my grandmother said.

My father turned to MacArthur and grew serious. "Never forget that a gun is always loaded."

MacArthur nodded.

"And what else?" my father said to MacArthur.

"Never point a gun at someone unless you mean to kill him," MacArthur said.

"Excuse me," my mother said, moving near the table. "Are you sure all of this is quite safe?" Her hands wavered above the bowl of gunpowder.

"That's right," my grandmother said. "Couldn't something blow up here?"

My father and MacArthur seemed to have been hoping for this question. They led us outside for a demonstration, MacArthur following behind my father with the bowl of powder and a box of matches. "Gunpowder is not like gasoline in a tank," my father said. He tipped a line of powder onto the sidewalk.

"It's not like wheat in a silo, either," MacArthur said, handing the matches to my father.

"Everybody stand back," my father said as he touched a match to the powder. It flared up with a hiss and gave off a stream of pungent smoke.

We watched the white smoke curl into the branches of our pecan tree, and then my grandmother said, "Well, it surely is a pleasure to learn that the house can burn down without blowing up."

Even my father laughed. On the way back into the house, he grew magnanimous and said to me, "You can learn to load shells, too, you know."

"No, thanks," I said. "My destiny is with the baton." I was practicing to be a majorette. It was the white tasseled boots I was after, and the pink lipstick. Years later, a woman friend, seeing a snapshot of me in the white-braided costume, a sort of paramilitary outfit with ruffles, said, "What a waste of your youth, what a corruption of your womanhood." Today, when I contemplate my wasted youth and corrupted womanhood, I recall that when I left high school I went to college. When MacArthur left high school, he went to war.

It is nine years after the gunpowder lesson, and I am a graduate student teaching a section of freshman composition at a large university. On a bright June day, at the end of the school year, one of my students, a Vietnam veteran, offers to give me a present of a human ear. We are walking under a long row of trees after the last class of the term and moving into the dark, brilliant shadows of the trees, then again into the swimming light of the afternoon. We are two weeks short of the solstice, and the sun has never seemed so bright. The student slides his book bag from his shoulder and says, "I would like to give you a present for the end of the course."

Ahead of us, the plane trees are so uniformly spaced, so beautifully arched that they form a green arcaded cloister along the stone walk. A soft, easing wind passes through the boughs with the sound of falling water. "Don't get me wrong," he says. "But I'd like to give you an ear."

Did he know that I came from a military family? Did he know that I had a nineteen-year-old brother in Vietnam? Did he know that my sense of the war derived largely from the color snapshots MacArthur had sent of happy young men posed before the Army's largest movable artillery weapon, their boots heavy with red dust, the jungle rising like a green temple behind them? There were two things MacArthur asked me to send him during his thirteen-month tour—marinated artichoke hearts and Rolling Stones tapes. The only artichoke hearts I could find came in glass jars and were not permitted in the Army's mailbags. The first Stones tapes I sent were washed away in a monsoon flood. I sent more tapes. These were stolen by an old man who wanted to sell them on the black market. I sent more Stones tapes.

These MacArthur gave to a wounded boy who was being airlifted to a hospital in Tokyo.

It has been said that the war in Vietnam was so fully photographed that it was the one war we learned the truth about. Which truth did we learn, and who learned it? One of the most famous pictures to come out of the war was the videotape of the South Vietnam chief of police firing a bullet into the head of a prisoner, a man who stood before the chief in shorts and a loose plaid shirt. He looked the chief in the eye, looked with fear and no hope, and was still looking with fear and no hope in that moment when he was already dead but had not yet fallen like a rag into the Saigon street. There were other memorable pictures like that. There were also ones like the picture of the blond, blue-eyed soldier, his head wrapped becomingly in a narrow bandage ("Just a flesh wound, sir"), reaching toward the camera as if to summon help for his wounded comrade. This photograph, with its depiction of handsome, capable, white middle-class goodwill, was so popular that it appeared in every major American news source and has been republished many times since, whenever a news agency wants to do a story on the Vietnam era.

That picture always reminds me of my student, a man in his late twenties who had served three tours of duty in Vietnam and was being put through college by the Army so that he could return to active duty as an officer—the student who stood before me pulling a canvas sack from his book bag on that dazzling June day at the end of my first year as a teacher.

"Don't get me wrong," the student said. "But I would like to give you an ear."

"What would you want to do that for?"

"I want to give you a present. I want to give you something for the end of the course." He withdrew his hand from the sack and opened it, palm up.

You probably have heard about the ears they brought back with them from Vietnam. You may have heard how the ears were carried in pouches or worn like necklaces, the lobes perforated so that they could be threaded on a leather thong. You may have heard that the ears looked like dried fruit, or like seashells, or like leaves curling beneath an oak tree. The mind will often make a metaphor when it cannot make anything else.

A human ear, though, still looks like a human ear. It is only after you have stared at it for a long while, at its curving ridges and shallow basins, that you begin to see: here is the dry bed of a wide river valley, here is the tiny village, the bright paddy, the water buffalo. Here is the world so green you could taste that green-

ness on your tongue even from an altitude of ten thousand feet in a jet bomber.

As the student and I looked at each other in the
sunlight, two young women strolling along the walk
separated in order to pass us—parted like river water
moving around an island. They were laughing and did
not notice what the student held in his hand. "So," said
one of the women, "my mother calls me back to say they
had to put the poor dog to sleep, and you know what she
says?" The student and I turned to hear what the
mother had said. "She says, 'And you know, Anita, that
dog's mind was still good. He wasn't even senile.' "

When the student turned back to me, he was smiling. "What a world," he said. He extended his hand.

"Thank you," I said. "But I do not want that
present."

We had begun to move again. I was walking
slowly, trying to show with my easy pace that I was not
afraid. Perhaps he was angry with me for something I
had said in class. Perhaps he was on drugs.

"It's okay," he said, "I have lots more."

"Really," I said. "No, but thank you."

"If you don't want this one, I can give you a better
one." He reached into the bag again.

"How can you tell which is which?" I said calmly,

as if I were inquiring about fishing lures or nuts and bolts or types of flower seed.

"I can tell," he said. "I've got this one memorized. This one's a girl." The girl, he told me, was thirteen. At first, the men in his outfit had taken pity on her and given her food and cigarettes. Then they learned that she was the one who planted mines around their encampment in the night.

It took us a long time to cross the campus and shake hands and say good-bye. Two days later, the student left a bottle of vodka on my desk while I was out. Apparently he had been sincere in wanting to give me a present. I never saw the student again. I did not see another war souvenir of that kind until after my brother returned from Vietnam.

The autumn we lived at Fort Sill, our family ate five hundred doves. There was a fifty-day dove season, a ten-dove limit each day. Every night, my mother brought the birds to the table in a different guise. They were baked and braised and broiled. They were basted and stuffed, olive-oiled and gravied. But there were too many of them, each tiny and heart-shaped, the breastbone prominent in outline even under a sauce. Finally, a platter of doves was set before us and MacArthur said,

"I am now helping myself to a tuna casserole. There is cheese in this casserole, and some cracker crumbs." He passed the platter to me. "And what are you having, Gemma?"

"I am having jumbo shrimps," I said. "And some lemon."

In this way, the platter moved around the table. My mother was having lamb. My grandmother was having pork chops. My father hesitated before he took the meat fork. All his life, he had been shooting game for the dinner table. He believed he was teaching his family a lesson in economy and his son a lesson in wilderness survival. No one had ever made a joke about these meals. He looked at MacArthur. Although my father had never said it, MacArthur was exactly the kind of son he had hoped to have—tall and good-natured, smart and obedient, a boy who could hit a bull's-eye on a paper target with his .22 rifle. "All right," my father said at last. "I'm having a steak."

However, after dinner he said, "If you want to play a game, let's play a real game. Let's play twenty questions." He took a pen from his pocket and flattened a paper napkin to use as a scorecard. He looked at MacArthur. "I am thinking of something. What is it?" We were all going to play this game, but my father's look implied that MacArthur was the principal opponent.

MacArthur tried to assume the gamesman's bland expression. "Is it animal?" he said.

My father appeared to think for a while. He mused at the candles. He considered the ceiling. This was part of the game, trying to throw the opponents off the trail. "Yes, it is animal."

"Is it a toad?" my grandmother said.

"No, no," MacArthur said. "It's too soon to ask that."

"It certainly is not a toad," my father said. He made a great show of entering a mark against us on the napkin. This was another part of the game, trying to rattle the opponents by gloating.

"Is it bigger than a breadbox?" my mother said.

"Yes."

"Is it bigger than a car?" I said.

"Yes."

"Is it bigger than a house?" MacArthur said.

"Yes."

"Is it the Eiffel Tower?" my grandmother said.

Again my father used exaggerated motions to record the mark. MacArthur dropped his head into his arms. This was an unmanly response.

"Settle down," my father said. "Think."

"Can't we play some other game?" my grand-mother said. "This game is never any fun."

"We are not trying to have fun," my father said. "We are trying to use our minds."

So the game went, until we had used up our twenty no answers, and my father revealed the thing he had been thinking of. The thing was "the rocket's red glare"—the light from exploded gunpowder. Gunpowder, if you analyzed its ingredients, was actually animal, vegetable, *and* mineral—providing you agreed that the carbon component could be derived from animal sources. He poured a drink and leaned back to tell us a story. The first time he had played the game he was a soldier on a ship going to England. The ship was in one of the largest convoys ever to cross the Atlantic during the Second World War. The sea was rough. German submarines were nearby. Some men got sea-sick, and everyone was nervous. They began to play games, and they played one game of twenty questions for two days. That was the game whose answer was "the rocket's red glare." My father had thought that one up.

That was as close as he ever came to telling us a war story. He had gone from England to Normandy Beach and later to the Battle of the Bulge, but when he remembered the war for us he remembered brave, high-spirited men not yet under attack. When he had finished speaking, he looked at his glass of scotch as the true drinker will—as if it contains a prophecy.

The spring following the season in which we ate whole generations of doves, MacArthur acquired two live chicks. A Woolworth's in the town near the post was giving chicks away to the first hundred customers in the door the Saturday before Palm Sunday. MacArthur was the first customer through the door and also the fifty-seventh. He named the chicks Harold and Georgette. He made big plans for Harold and Georgette. He was going to teach them how to walk a tightrope made of string and ride a chicken-sized Ferris wheel.

A week later, Harold and Georgette were eaten by our cat while we were at church. The chicks had been living in an open cardboard box on top of the refrigerator. No one imagined that a cat as fat and slothful as Al Bear would hurl himself that high to get an extra meal.

Looking at the few pale feathers left in the box, MacArthur said, "He ate them whole. He even ate the beaks."

"Poor chicks," my mother said.

"They were making an awful lot of noise up

there," my grandmother said. "They should have kept those beaks shut."

Everyone looked to see if MacArthur was crying. In our family, people believed that getting through a hardship intact was its own reward. "This is nothing to be upset about," my father said. "This is the way nature works." It was in the natural order of things for cats to eat birds, he told us. Even some birds ate other birds. Some animals ate cats. Everything we ate had once been alive. Wasn't a steak part of a steer? MacArthur looked away just long enough to roll his eyes at me. My father began to gesture and to project his voice. Now he was lecturing on the principles of Darwinian selection. He used the phrase "nature red in tooth and claw." He seemed to like that phrase, and used it again. The third time he said, "nature red in tooth and claw," Al Bear walked up behind him and threw up on the floor, all the little bird parts of Harold and Georgette still recognizable on the linoleum.

MacArthur never became a hunter of birds. By the time he turned twelve, and was given a shotgun for his birthday, we were stationed in Italy. The Italians, always a poor people, would shoot a bird out of a tree or blast one on the ground to get a meal. They had gone through

entire species of game birds this way and were now
working on the German songbirds that flew south for the
winter. Thus, the misfortunes of the Italian economy
allowed my brother to turn from real birds to imitation
ones. Soon after his birthday, he was taken to the skeet
range at Camp Darby, where he was permitted to shoot
fifty rounds at black-and-yellow disks, called pigeons.
Fifty recoils of a large gun are a lot for a boy, even one
big for his age, like MacArthur. By the time he got home
that day, there were bruises beginning to bloom across
his shoulder.

"Maybe he should wait until he's older," my
mother said.

"What ever happened to the all-American sports?"
my grandmother said. "Couldn't he learn to throw or
kick something?"

Months later, when we all drove into the post to see
him shoot in his first tournament, MacArthur kept saying, "See Kid MacArthur forget to load the gun. Watch
fake birds fall whole to the earth." "Kid MacArthur"
was what he called himself when something went wrong.
He did not like the general whose name he bore. He did
not admire him, as my parents did, for being the man
who said, "I shall return." MacArthur was not one of
those ordinary names, like John or Joan, which you

could look up in my grandmother's *Dictionary of Christian Appellations.* MacArthur was a name my brother had to research. General MacArthur, he decided, had talked a big game but then allowed his entire air force to be bombed on the ground the day after Pearl Harbor. General MacArthur had sent his troops into Bataan but had not sent along the trucks that carried food for the battalions. The general had fled to Australia, uttering his famous words, leaving his men to perish in the Death March.

"You'll be fine if you don't look out any windows," my father said. "Looking out the window" was his expression for allowing the mind to wander. "I'm pulling down all the shades on my windows," MacArthur said. "I'm battening all the hatches in my head."

Something overtook MacArthur when the tournament got under way and he finally stepped onto the range, the only boy among the shooters. The bones of his face grew prominent. His eyes became opaque, like the eyes of a man who can keep a secret. By the second time around the stations, he was third among the five shooters. No one spoke, except a man named Mr. Dimple, who was an engineer working for the American government in Italy, and the only civilian on the skeet range.

"That gosh-damned sun," Mr. Dimple said. "Those gosh-damned trees." It was a hot, bright day, and the angle of the sun made it difficult to see the disks as they sailed in front of a pine forest at the back of the range.

"Maybe we need a fence in front of those trees," Mr. Dimple said. After his next two shots, he said, "Damned if the wind didn't get to those birds before I did." It was clear that Mr. Dimple was disgracing himself before the cream of the American Army. When he spoke, the other men looked at the grass. The women, seated behind the semicircular range, looked at each other. Their eyes seemed to say, "Our men are not going to complain about any trees. Our men are not going to complain about the wind or the sun."

"I'm not wearing the right sunglasses," Mr. Dimple said.

MacArthur stepped up to the station just in front of the viewing area and called for the pigeons. "Pull!" Swinging to his right, he aimed just ahead of the flying, spinning disk. He pulled the first trigger and began the swing back to his left to get the second sailing bird before it touched the ground. The first bird exploded in a star of fragments and fell to the earth with the sound of raining gravel. The second bird fell untouched and landed on the ground with a *clack* as it struck another unexploded bird. Perhaps because his swing back had seemed so sure, so exactly timed, MacArthur could not believe he had missed. He shook his head as he stepped away from the station.

My father looked over at him and said within hearing of everyone on the range, "Whenever you step back from that peg, you step back the same way, hit or miss. You do not shake your head."

Mr. Dimple put his hand on his hip and sighed at his gun. Colonel McGrath and Major Solman looked away.

"Do you understand?"

MacArthur did understand. He was embarrassed. "Yes, sir," he said. As the group moved to the next station, the other men nodded at my father and gave MacArthur friendly punches on the arm. He was not going to grow up to be a Mr. Dimple.

The next year, MacArthur won a place on the championship team my father took to Naples. For years, my father liked to tell about MacArthur's first day on the range. "He was black-and-blue all over," my father said. "But he never spoke a word of complaint."

Two years later, we returned to the States to live on a post on Governors Island, which was in the middle of New York Harbor and so close to the Statue of Liberty that we could see her torchlight from our bedroom windows. It was on Governors Island that my father received a letter from the government that seemed to imply that MacArthur might not be an American citizen, because he had been born in the Philippines. He was not quite a foreigner, either, because his parents had been born in Ohio.

"He's a juvenile delinquent, is what he is," my grandmother said one day when my father was trying to explain the citizenship difficulty. She had slipped into MacArthur's room and found a cache of cigarette lighters. "Where does a fourteen-year-old boy get enough money to buy these things?" she said. "What does he do with them, anyway?"

"He doesn't smoke," I said, although I knew that with my father the health issue would not be the central one.

My mother beheld the lighters with great sadness. "I'll have a talk with him tonight."

"No one will speak to him yet," my father said. He was troubled because the evidence of MacArthur's criminality had been gathered in a kind of illegal search and seizure.

"Does this mean that MacArthur can never become president of the United States?" I said. In our family, we had been taught that if children were scrupulously honest, and also rose from their seats when strangers entered the room, and said "Yes, sir" and "No, sir" at the appropriate moments, and then went on to get a college education, they could grow up to be anything, including president of the United States. Even a woman could be president, if she kept her record clean and also went to college.

No one smiled at my joke.

The document my father held seemed to suggest that even though MacArthur was the son of patriots, someone somewhere might question the quality of his citizenship. It was a great blow to learn that he might be a thief as well as a quasi foreigner.

The document was a letter from the judge advocate of the post advising that foreign-born children be interviewed by the Department of Naturalization and Immigration. It also advised that they attend a ceremony in which they would raise their right hands, like ordinary immigrants, and renounce any residual loyalty to the countries of their births. It did not "require" that they do these things but it did "strongly recommend" that they do so. We never learned why the government made its strong recommendation, but there was something in the language of the letter that allowed one to think that foreign birth was like a genetic defect that could be surgically altered—it was like an extra brain that could be lopped off. (A communist brain! A socialist brain! The brain that would tell the hand to raise the gun against American democracy.)

"What were you doing in his chest of drawers?" my father said.

"I was dusting," my grandmother said.

"You were dusting the contents of a brown sack?"

"This would never have happened in Ohio," my grandmother said. "If we lived in Ohio, he would already be a citizen and would not have to hang around that neighborhood after school."

"In this house, we do not take other people's possessions without asking."

"That's the point." My grandmother picked up a lighter with each hand. "These *are* other people's possessions."

It was dark when I slipped out to intercept MacArthur. At night, it was always a surprise to ascend the slope of the post golf course and come upon a vision of New York City standing above the harbor, the lights of Wall Street rising like fire into the sky, all the glory and fearfulness of the city casting its spangled image back across the water to our becalmed and languorous island. If you looked away from the light of the city, you looked back into the darkness of the last three centuries, across roofs of brick buildings built by the British and the Dutch. The post was a Colonial retreat, an administrative headquarters, where soldiers strolled to work under the boughs of hardwood trees, and the trumpetings of the recorded bugle drifted through the leaves like a mist. It was a green, antique island, giving its last year of service to the United States Army.

My grandmother never boarded the ferry for Manhattan without believing that her life or, at the very least, the quality of her character was in peril. She did not like New Yorkers. They were grim and anxious. They had bad teeth. They did not live in a place where parents told their children that if they bit into an apple and found a worm, they would know that they were just getting a little extra protein.

"About how many do you think she took?" MacArthur said to me.

"She took about exactly all of them."

His face went slack. He still did not have that implacable expression that was supposed to help you through any crisis. "I was going to hock those on Monday to get some more cash for Christmas."

"By Monday, you will be restricted to quarters. By Monday, you will be calling your friends to tell them you can't go to any movies or parties over the holidays." I handed him a lighter. "I don't think they've got them counted," I said. The others were still lying on the dining table.

He was grateful for that lighter. "Thanks," he said. "This is the best one."

"How about a light?" I said. I opened a pack of my father's cigarettes and took one out.

He snapped open the lighter and ignited it so deftly that the whole movement looked like a magic trick. "This is what we learn to do at P.S. 104," he said.

Neither of us smoked, but we inflicted the cigarette upon ourselves with relish, exhaling fiercely into the raw night air. "I'm not asking where you got them, of course," I said.

He smiled. "I won almost every one of them throwing dice and playing cards. At lunch everybody goes out to steal, and after school everybody plays for the loot. Remember me? Kid Competition. I'm great at games."

"That's a story you could probably tell them," I said.

He ground the cigarette out under his foot. "Look at me," he said. "I'm littering Army property." Then he said, "I did steal a couple of them. Either you steal, and you're one of guys, or you don't steal, and you're a sleazo and everybody wants to fight."

He was very tall by then. The bones close to his skin—his wrist bones, knees, shoulder bones—looked as though they had been borrowed from a piece of farm machinery. If you were as big as he was and also the new kid at school, someone would always want to fight you. We had started walking and were now on the dark side of Governors Island, standing by the seawall that looked toward the small lights of Brooklyn. The wind was blowing at our backs from the west, bringing the sharp, oily smell from the New Jersey refineries, but we could also smell the salt and fish taste of the ocean, and for a moment I could imagine us far away from every city and every Army post and every rural town we had ever known. He leaned across the railing of the seawall and looked tired. He had posed for himself an even more demanding ideal than the family had, and he was humiliated to perceive himself as a thief.

"Look," I said. "Just tell them you bought a couple of lighters with your lunch money to get the stake for the gambling." He nodded toward the water without conviction. "Don't ruin Christmas for yourself."

"Okay, I won't."

The next day he volunteered the truth to my father and was not only restricted to quarters but also made to go uptown to meet the victims of the crimes. My father wore his uniform, with the brass artilleryman's insignia, two cannons crossed under a missile. MacArthur wore the puffy green jacket and the green hat that had inspired his friends to call him the Jolly Green Giant. They were a gift from my mother and grandmother, so he had to wear them. They made him look like a lumbering asparagus stalk, a huge vegetable king, who could be spotted on any subway platform or down any length of city blocks. At each store, he removed his green hat and made a speech of apology, then returned one or several of the lighters. Since the lighters were now used, he also paid for them out of his Christmas-shopping money. It hurt him to be the one who had nothing to give on Christmas morning. And at school he was an outcast.

"I am now Kid Scum," he said. "The Jolly Green Creep."

He got a Certificate of Citizenship, though, and when he entered the Army, four years later, he went in as a real American.

On MacArthur's last day of leave before he left for Vietnam, we drove him to the Cleveland airport and then stood like potted palms behind the plate-glass window of the terminal building. My father had retired from the Army by then, and the family had returned to Ohio.

"He ought to love the heat," my grandmother said. "He was born in the heat."

"He's a smart soldier," my father said. "It's the smart men who are most likely to get through any war." My father had always believed in smartness as other people believe in amulets.

The plane began to move, and we strained to find MacArthur's face in one of the small windows. "There he is," my mother said. "I see his hand in the window."

A woman standing next to her said, "No, that's our son. See how big that hand is?"

The woman's husband said, "Our son was a linebacker at Ohio State. He weighs two hundred and sixty-five pounds."

"He's a good boy," the woman said, and we all nodded, as if it were obvious that physical size could be a measure of a person's character.

After we left the turnpike and drove south to the fertile, rolling land of the Killbuck Valley, which had never produced a war protester, my grandmother said, "I believe in Vietnam." She emphasized the word *be-*

lieve, as if Vietnam were a denomination of the Christian faith. In the 1950s, she had been a member of something called the Ground Observer Corps. Members of the Corps scanned the skies with binoculars, looking for Russian aircraft. At that time she lived in a small Ohio town whose major industries were a bus-seat factory and an egg-noodle plant. Twice a month she stood on the roof of the high school to keep these vital industries safe from a communist air attack.

"I believe in luck," I said. "I believe the Jolly Green Giant's luck will get him through. Remember how he always won at bingo?"

"We took care of the Japs and the Jerries," my grandmother said. "We held off the pinkos in Korea."

"I do not think that any pinkos are planning to invade the United States," I said.

"You've got a lot to learn," my mother said. "They're already here."

"When you get back to school, I do not want to hear that you are marching in those protests," my father said.

I was already marching, but that was a secret. "Isn't this the place where we notice the grass?" I said.

When my father was still in the Army, we spent all of his leave time going back to the Killbuck Valley. As we crossed the state line and drew closer to the valley where the Killbuck River ran and all of our relatives lived, my father would say, "Doesn't anyone notice that the grass is getting greener?" We used to say, "Naw, this grass looks like any other grass." We made a joke of the grass, but we all did love the look of that land. On some level, the grasses of the Killbuck Valley, the clover, timothy, alfalfa, the corn, wheat, and oats, the dense woods of the hills, the freshwater springs, and the shivering streams—all of this was connected with the necessity of a standing Army. It was as if my father had said, "This is what we will fight for."

MacArthur had been out of the Army for a year, and his life seemed defined by negatives—no job, no college, no telephone, no meat. He lived alone in a rented farmhouse deep in the Killbuck Valley, about twenty miles from the town where the family had settled.

"He comes every other Sunday and all he eats is the salad or the string beans," my grandmother said to me. The soul of our family life always hovered over the dinner table, where we renewed the bond of our kinship over game and steaks and chops and meatloaf. My parents and grandmother perceived MacArthur's new diet both as a disease and as a mark of failing character.

When they went to visit, they took along a roast or a ten-pound bag of hamburger.

"See what you can find out," my mother said. I was home for Christmas week and on my way out to see him. "Talk to him. See if he has any plans."

He did not have any plans. What he had was a souvenir of the war just like the one my student had tried to give me on that June day under the trees. This one was tucked into a small padded envelope lying on the kitchen table. The envelope made me curious, and I kept reaching out to finger the ragged edges of brown paper as we drank a pot of tea. MacArthur, sitting on the kitchen counter because there was only one chair, finally said, "Go ahead. Look." I opened the envelope and looked. There was a moment then when the winter sun was like heavy metal in the room, like something that could achieve critical mass if a question mark sparked the air. For some reason, I thought of the young woman reporting what her mother had said about the dead dog—"And you know, that dog's mind was still good. He wasn't even senile." I thought of what I had wanted to say to my student that day: "I didn't think that something like this could look exactly like itself so much later and so far away."

"That's not mine," MacArthur said. "That belongs

to Dixon." His face was as flat as pond ice, and I saw that at last he had achieved the gamesman's implacable expression. Even in the long curves of his body there was something that said that nothing could startle or move him.

"Who's Dixon?" I said.

"Oh, you know who he is. My friend the space cadet. The one in the V.A. hospital."

"The one from Oklahoma." Now I remembered Dixon from the snapshots. He was the one who glued chicken feathers to his helmet.

"This is his idea of a great Christmas present," MacArthur said.

His eyes were so still and wide I could see the gold flecks in them. He looked away, looked down at his legs dangling from the counter, and I suddenly felt the solitariness of that rented farmhouse in the Killbuck Valley, the hills and fields hardened under snow, the vegetable garden rutted with ice. When I stood up to touch his arm, he did not move or speak. He seemed to have escaped from me in an evaporation of heat. Even in my imagination, I could not go where he had gone. All I knew was that somewhere in the jungle had been a boy named Dixon, a boy from Oklahoma, who had grown up on land just like the land my father used to hunt while MacArthur trailed behind with bright-red boxes of homemade ammunition. But now Dixon was a nut who sent ears through the mail, and MacArthur was unemployed and living alone in the country.

Suddenly the ear was back in the envelope Dixon had sent it in, and MacArthur was saying, "I'm sorry, but I don't have much around here you'd like to eat."

Later, we stood out back where the garden was and looked at the corn stubble and broken vines. MacArthur paced the rows and said, "These are my snap beans. These are my pumpkins." He proceeded past carrots, beets, onions, turnips, cabbages, and summer squash, looking at each old furrow with a stalwart affection, as if the plants he named would bloom in snow when they heard him speak.

"They asked me to find out what you plan for the future," I said.

"Oh, great." He kicked a hump of snow. "Did you ever notice how with the family your life is always a prospective event? 'When you're a little older, when you grow up, when you get old just like me'?" He relaxed again and dropped an arm across my shoulders. "I'm just a carpenter now. Let me show you my lights." I thought he meant lamps, since most of his rooms were empty except for secondhand lamps standing in corners.

He was restoring the house for its owner, to work off the rent. In the front room, he said, "Now we are going to play a game. Tell me what you see. All right? Do you get it? Tell me what you see."

"I see an old iron floor lamp."

"No, tell me about the *light*. What kind of light do you see?" The walls were freshly painted white, but the sun had moved around the house, so the room was growing dark. I fumbled for a proper answer.

"Eggshell light?" I said.

He made a great show of entering an imaginary mark on an imaginary napkin in his hand. "Nooooo," he said. "It certainly is not eggshell light."

Then I understood, and I laughed. "Is it animal light?"

"Settle down, now. Use your head."

"Is it vegetable light?"

He surveyed the room, its greens, and blue-greens and ochers, the pale colors of a northern room at the end of the day. "Yes, I think you could call this vegetable light. Maybe *eggplant* light." He laughed and wadded up the imaginary napkin.

We moved through the house then, making up ridiculous names for the light we saw. We found moose light, and hippopotamus light, and potato-chip light. We found a violet light we named after our cousin Neilon's purple car, and an orange light we called Aunt Sheila's Hair, and a silver light we called Uncle Dave, after the silver dollars he used to send us on our birthdays. We returned to the kitchen, with its wide reach of western windows, and saw the red light of the sunset splayed across the cabinets. "Oh, yes," MacArthur said. "And here we have another light. Here we have a light just like the light of the rocket's red glare."

The sun had dropped below the tree line when he went to turn on his lamps, and I put on my coat. "Well, I have to go," I said. "I'll keep writing. I'll come see you the next time I'm back."

He walked me to the car, holding my arm as I slipped over the pebbly snow. We stopped to look at the western sky, now furrowed with that fierce red you see at that time of year when there are ice crystals in the air. All the things nearby had become brilliant black silhouettes—the stand of trees to our right, the boarded-up barn, the spiky fragments of the garden. The sky grew fiercer and gave off a light I could not name.

"The shortest day of the year," MacArthur said. He reached into his jacket and withdrew the brown envelope. "Take this," he said.

He held it out, and this time, because he was my

brother, I said, "All right," and took it. I hugged him and got in the car. I knew he was not going to be home for Christmas. "You're going all the way to Oklahoma to see Dixon, aren't you?"

He had already started back to the house and had to turn to face me with his surprise.

"Remember me?" I said. "I'm the Kid's sister. I'll think of something to tell them at home."

"Thanks," he said.

When I got to the bottom of the lane, I stopped the car to wave. He had come back through the house and was standing on the dark porch, legs evenly spaced, like a soldier at ease, the gold light of his house swooning in every window. Before I drove off, I slipped the envelope under the front seat with the road maps, thinking that someday I would remove it and decide what to do.

It was still there five years later, when I sold the car. During those five years, my father, always a weekend drinker, began to drink during the week. My grandmother broke her hip in a fall. My mother, a quiet woman, was now helped through her quiet by Valium. MacArthur finished restoring his rooms and moved to another farmhouse, in a different county. Finally, he took a job as a cook—a breakfast cook, doing mostly eggs and pancakes—and in this way continued to be a person without plans.

The boy I sold the car to was just eighteen years old and wanted to go west to California. He was tall, like my brother, and happy to be managing his own life at last. The cuffs of his plaid flannel shirt had shrunk past his wrists, and, seeing his large wrist bones exposed to the cold bright air, I liked him immediately.

"Are you sure you're charging me enough for this?" Leaning under the hood, he looked like a construction crane. "This is one of the best engines Ford ever made," he said. "Whooee!"

"Believe me. I'm charging you a good price."

He wanted to celebrate the purchase and buy me a drink. "I bet this old Betsy has some stories to tell." He winked at me. He could not believe his good luck, and he was flirting. The cold spring air seemed to take the shape of a promise, but then there was still the problem of the envelope under the front seat. In five years, I had removed it several times. I had thought of bureau drawers and safe-deposit boxes. I had even thought of getting Dixon's address and sending it back. Again and again, I slid it under the seat once more unopened.

"Come on," the boy said. "Let's have a drink and tell some stories."

"Really, I can't," I said. "I have to go somewhere." I didn't want to get to know him. I had meant to retrieve the envelope before I turned over the car, but, standing on the curb, signing the pink slip, I discovered it would be easier just to leave it there.

"Hey," the boy said. "Look what you did. You made a sheep."

"What?" I said.

"You made a sheep with your breath. Hey—there, you did it again." Now I tried to see what he had seen in the frosty air, but it was gone. He gave me the money, we shook hands, and he got in the car. "Not many people can make a whole sheep," he said. He turned the key. "Most folks just puff out a part of a sheep."

"Wait," I said.

He put the car back in neutral and leaned out the window. "You change your mind? You hop in and I'll take you to Mr. Mike's Rock-and-Roll Heaven."

"No," I said. "I have to tell you something. There's something I didn't tell you about the car."

He stopped smiling, because he must have thought I hadn't given him a good price after all—that there was a crack in the engine block or a dogleg in the frame.

"Well, what the heck is it? Just lay me out then. The last car I had broke down on me in three weeks." He was remorseful now and disappointed in both of us.

I paused a long time. "I just think I should tell you that this car takes premium gas."

He was happy again. "Shoot, I knew that," he said. He put the car back into gear.

"You be careful," I said. "You have a good trip."

He gave me the thumbs-up sign and edged away from the curb, looking both ways, in case there was traffic.

I liked that boy. I wanted him to get safely to California and find a good life and fall in love and father a large brood of cheerful people who would try to give you too much for a used car and would always wear their shirtsleeves too short. I watched him drive away and around the corner. I started back to the house but then turned to look at the cloud of exhaust that hung in the air. I wanted to see what figure it made. I wanted to see if it would be a sheep or a part of a sheep or a person or something else, and what I saw instead, before it unfurled into the maple trees, was a thin banner of pale smoke.

*T*his is it: life lived in a holding pattern because the landing gear won't go down, and Megan sips wine trying to think of jokes to crack; brave, witty exit lines. She has a husband, George, who has lost the art of conversation and never comes to their bedroom until she is asleep and talking in strange languages. This morning he told her that last night she said three times, quite distinctly, "The mummy orders enchiladas." She has a good friend named Vera, running on hormones and Valium and a fear of all natural phenomena (the two minor earthquake tremors in the last five weeks, for example), who called her at work this morning with a luncheon invitation, saying, "There's something I have to talk to you about," to which Megan replied, "I have a business lunch," lying, because words are like eggs—they can hatch into creatures with lives of their own, the dove, the partridge, the yellow-winged oriole, singing sweet songs, but also the hawk, the eagle, the condor, tearing flesh away from the bones.

Instead at noon she left the industrial park where she works and drove west until she found a fast-food place selling overtenderized steaks—DES, BHT, and monosodium glutamate. The truth is: it tastes good and life is short. Megan has lost twelve pounds in the last month on George's fish-and-vegetable diet. A few moments ago, passing herself in the plate-glass window, she agreed with herself that she was a person made too thin by good advice.

She ignores the salad, eats the steak, and sips the wine, and thinks about the embattled brain cells, how at this moment a thousand of them are turning over on their backs and sticking their little feet in the air. She smiles (always her own best audience) and now an old woman in a stylish hat, mistaking the smile for an invitation, takes the seat opposite. She says that she lives two blocks away in the Sunset Tower Senior Home and can never get a decent meal there.

"The dietician is shocking," she says. "Some people get hors d'oeuvres before the meals and others of us do not." The woman is an immigrant. She says she has no family except for a son in Sacramento who visits only every other month. Her roommate is a thief. She, the old woman, has written a note to the counselor, listing her grievances. She pulls the note from her purse and hands it to Megan, who reads as she chews: "My roommate disrupts my things. I am suspect her of losing some of them, especially my toothpaste. I am frightened of her because she also interferes with my other things. In doing this she undermines my very poor health condition."

Megan shakes her head sympathetically. What can she do?

"When I show this note to the counselor, the counselor says, 'I think you get upset over a minor thing. Try to work it out.' "

Megan shakes her head again.

"There's no protection. She stole my perfume, too. She doesn't use it. I can only think she can throw it away."

"How terrible," Megan says.

"If I live there for longer I will die."

Neither of them is eating now. The old woman stares at Megan with sudden indignation, as if Megan were the counselor who doesn't understand, and then she picks up her tray and moves to another table.

The mummy orders enchiladas.

Everybody has problems.

Megan stands at the window with a cup of coffee and a cigarette while George does sit-ups on the carpet. He jerks three times before he reclines again on the floor.

Ah-pouf-pouf-pouf. George has got a sort of dance rhythm going with his breathing. George, Megan wants to say, I know what you're doing. You're making yourself into a person who has nothing to do with me.

For the last three months George has been remodeling himself along lines suggested by certain consumer bulletins and TV shows. He gave up beer and started sucking on licorice roots. He gave up meat and started lifting weights. He shaved his armpits in the manner of championship lifters on "Wide World of Sports." *Pouf-ah. Pouf-ah.* George snatched and heaved on the exhale, contemplating his own mortality.

"George," Megan said. "I do not want to go to the beach this summer with a man in naked armpits."

His stomach flattened out. His arms and legs, once lanky and limber, took on the stiff glistening promise of a new topography. "George," she said, amusing only herself, "you think Arnold Schwarzenegger is sexy? Arnold Schwarzenegger gets a rash where his big legs rub together."

Tonight for supper they had fish sticks, which had been out of the ocean too long and tasted like small punishments. Now she looks at the view that is the standard view that comes with all apartments-with-a-view south of San Francisco: telephone pole, four lanes of commuter traffic, some rooftops, more poles, and finally in the distance a glimpse of the mountains hiding the sea. On the telephone pole, only a few feet from the window, someone has nailed a sign that says that a cat is lost and his name is Le Max. (Here Le Max? Here Le Max?) This morning before she went to work Megan went down to the pole and read the fine print: two-time Santa Clara County champion, long hair, black Persian, very rare. Now she notices on the far side of the street, near the curb, a flat, treaded shape.

"George," she says. "Did you notice anything dead on the street when you came home from work?"

She turns to look at him. He is straining from the floor to touch his toes with his elbows, and he gives her a wild-eyed look to indicate that he can't talk until he gets to number five hundred. "Three ninety-six," he whispers. "Three ninety-seven."

Recently she inventoried the contents of the kitchen: eleven knives, nine forks, seven spoons, three bread pans, three cake pans. Somehow they have contrived to own only odd numbers of things, which will be difficult to divide down the middle.

George and Megan are seated on the sofa watching TV. His arm is draped fraternally over her shoulder. She snuggles against his side and tries to think of neutral topics. His job, her job, how much they have put away toward a down payment on a house. The Vista View complex is that kind of place—one where all the residents are waiting until they can touch down in a neighboring suburb and begin their real lives, planting geraniums and coaxing the grass green in the summer.

"I think I'll try to quit smoking again," she says. Actually, she hasn't given it much thought recently, but suddenly it seems an innovative idea, something she can do for herself and George. She waits for him to approve. He waves his hand to show that he wants to hear the program on TV, where a man is running across a rooftop. For some time now the spaces in their conversation have flourished. There is a parallel, in fact, between the diminution of their evening chitchat and the development of George's new body, as if words are some kind of fiber diet George is using to pack the hollows of his triceps.

At the commercial break she says, "How do you think I should go about quitting?"

George shrugs, his eyes still on the screen.

"I mean, what do you think the first step should be?"

"Just throw the damn things away," he says. "Use some discipline."

"That's a very good idea," she says, enthusiastically, as if George has just outlined a complex strategy and offered to collaborate on the invention of the new Megan.

When the program resumes the man is still running across the rooftop. He is dressed in black. He is the celebrated Cat Burglar of Paris, who steals from the rich and gives to the poor. Megan thinks of Le lost Max, a fugitive from the Vista View complex. Height, six inches. Weight, twelve pounds. Hair, black. Eyes, green. Presumed dead, but who knows? Maybe Le Max has faked his own suicide, assumed a new identity, and is even now padding across El Camino Real, heading for a nice life in the mountains. Good-bye, Max. Good luck.

Megan has not smoked a cigarette for two days and has been sucking on lemon drops instead. She tried one of George's licorice roots, but it was truly like eating a piece of a tree, too primeval. She has now eaten four bags of lemon drops, two bags a day, an extra four thousand calories of tooth rot, according to Vera's calculations. "Your lungs will be fine, but your teeth will fall out," Vera is saying. It is Saturday afternoon and they are walking along the shaded street of another suburb, looking for an empty lot Vera wants to photograph.

"First the gums go soft and gray like dirty sponges, and then the teeth let go."

"I know," Megan says. "I can feel them right now hanging on to the bone with their little fingers and crying for help."

Vera smiles but says, "It's not a joke. You should try carrots."

"You can't smoke carrots."

"I'm serious. Think of radishes. Think of celery."

"What am I eating already? Every day two big salads and some smelly fish." What she wants to say is, Vera, don't make me into a trivial, inferior person whom you can take lightly. What she says instead is, "Don't pick on me."

"This isn't picking. This is advice."

"Believe me, it's picking."

Vera pauses on the walk near a cascade of bougainvillea. Her eyes in the warm light are deep violet, dilated, beautiful. She looks at the walk and when she looks back up she has that nervous face Megan has seen so often that says nothing is safe—tuna fish can give you brain damage, bacon can give you cancer, hair dryers shoot asbestos filaments into your lungs and nose. "I'm the one who needs advice," she says. "I'm two weeks late."

"Why?" Megan says. What she means is why you? A year ago Megan had an ectopic pregnancy, a child growing in the wrong place. Now she has only one tube and an erratic ovary—automatic birth control. Twice she has driven Vera to a clinic and sat in the waiting room while Vera lay on an operating table and a fetus was torn from the walls of her womb, sucked through a transparent tube, and dropped into a stainless-steel pan.

"I can't help it," Vera says. "I'm always lonely."

"I don't want to hear about it."

"I can't use the pill or the IUD and I always forget my diaphragm."

"I really don't want to hear about it."

"It isn't what you think."

"I don't care."

They walk in silence until they find the empty lot, and Megan sits on the curb as Vera takes pictures with her Polaroid. Vera is an architectural renderer. She has vision. She can look at a few geometric shapes disposed around a scored sheet, and she can see an entire apartment complex, complete with trees, flowers, shrubs, people talking animatedly on the sidewalks, beach towels slung over their shoulders, tennis racquets in their hands, romance, marriage, and happy childhoods in their smiles. Vera's pictures look nothing like the Vista View complex, where the unshaded asphalt soaks up the heat, and people merely nod to each other as they take out the trash.

"Someone paid a lot of money to get this nice neighborhood rezoned for apartment buildings," Megan says as they walk back to the car.

"It's not that nice," Vera says. "Look at these stucco places, the architecture of the middle class." The architectural details, she says, are borrowed and phony and pretending to be too many things at once. There is a pointed arch taken from a Gothic cathedral and trivialized into a small front door. Here are some red Spanish tiles sitting on top of some fake half-timbering. There are two Greek columns attached to a Pueblo-style façade. What a joke, she says, what a laugh—buildings constructed out of fantasy and misinformation.

"They don't look so bad to me," Megan says and has a momentary vision of herself and George living in one of these places with a red wagon and plastic balls cluttering the front walk.

Vera drives badly as they return to the Vista View complex, braking at the on-ramp, then accelerating just as a truck bears down upon them. "You know how many men I've slept with in the last six weeks?" she says.

"I don't want to know."

"Six."

They ride in silence until they arrive at Megan's apartment, when Vera says, "I was thinking that maybe I should have this one. I was thinking that maybe I should give it to someone who would like it."

"That sounds like a dumb idea to me."

Seven o'clock on Monday morning and Megan drives George to the airport as small lies fly out of his mouth like hummingbirds.

"I wish I didn't have to go," he says. "I'd rather stay here."

George is afraid of planes. The prospect of falling wingless to the earth always makes him sentimental.

"I wish you didn't have to go, too. Sometimes I think thieves will break into the apartment." This is not true—she is just keeping the conversation circuits open, and now George reaches across the front seat and puts a hand on her thigh.

"It happens every day. They could tie you up and load everything into a truck. People would just think we were moving," he says. Megan nods. The Vista View complex is not a community but merely a collection of people who incidentally happen to share the geography of a parking lot and three identical buildings. "Los Angeles makes me tired," he says. "The smog makes me tired. I never get any exercise and I eat lousy food."

"It's only two days." George works for a computer company that is developing a new traffic-light system for a suburb of Los Angeles, one that will measure the flow of traffic every fifteen minutes, at four thousand intersections, and alter the rhythm of the signals accordingly. He makes these trips every two months and is buoyant when he returns—a man of intellect and power who manipulates an entire town.

"You'll probably be glad to have me out of the apartment for a while."

"No, I won't."

"You'll probably go out and eat tacos and smoke cigarettes."

"No, I won't." She smiles. "I'll wait until you get back."

"You know, I never actually said you had to eat what I eat."

"George, I was just joking."

"If you want to eat empty calories, that's fine with me. If you want to smoke and drink and sprinkle carcinogens on your breakfast cereal, okay."

"For heaven's sake. It was a joke."

The traffic is moving fast and easily—six lanes of commuters who know where they're going and drive to work on automatic pilot. George settles against his seat as if he's relaxing but says, "I have a knot in my stomach. There hasn't been a crash in a long time."

She wonders whether he's just computing odds with his engineer's mind and concluding that somewhere there is a plane with its number coming up, or whether he's afraid there's such a thing as a vengeful fury. She decides to launch a small weather balloon. "Vera," she says—using the word to test the air—"Vera," she says again, "wants to come over and cook us supper when you get back."

For a living Megan writes sentences. She works at a place called Comp Currics, Inc., which sells computerized educational programs to large school systems. The sentences she writes do not add up to little communities of paragraphs. They are fed randomly into a computer, which, through telephone hookups, feeds them to terminals in New York, St. Louis, Dallas, and Detroit, where students with low grades practice reading the English language. It is hard to write thousands of sentences that have nothing to do with each other and that must be very short, use a limited vocabulary, and make no references to forests, farms, streams, wildflowers, nuclear families, or anything else associated with country life or middle-class values. Megan is good at her job. The old man *sat* down on the park bench. The milk *sat* on the table too long. The woman *sat* up in bed.

Sometimes to keep herself awake she allows the sentences to follow a story line on her legal tablet, but for two days the stories have been going out of control.

> Karen *had* found a dead cat in the street.
> A strange man *had* followed Karen home.
> Karen *had* called the police.
> The police *had* not come.
> Karen's hair *had* touched the foot of the dead cat.
> Karen *had* worn a blue dress.
> The dress *had* belonged to her sister.
> The sister *had* died in an airplane crash.

Megan has just crumpled up three sheets of sentences and is now writing a letter to the owner of Le Max: Dear Unhappy Lost-Cat Owner, I regret to inform you that I have reason to believe that your valuable and beloved pet has been squashed by a passing car in front of the Vista View apartment complex. If you are the sort of person who always likes to know what's what, I imagine you will be grateful for this letter. If you are the sort of person who likes to be in doubt, I am sorry. Yours sincerely, A Resident.

Each of them knows Vera is pregnant, but no one mentions it. Vera and George drink Perrier water and Megan drinks wine, as the sauce simmers on the stove. They talk about Vera's apartment building, George's traffic system, and Megan's language arts project. Everyone agrees that everyone else is working hard. Megan and Vera return to the kitchen to wash the lettuce, and George watches the news. Megan starts on the salad dressing, and Vera goes back to the living room. She and George stand at the window and discuss the prospects for an earthquake. They sound as if they are discussing the stock market.

"The San Andreas fault looks bad. The Calaveras looks bad, too."

Megan steps out of the kitchen for a moment and observes the way they are standing, George's elbow just brushing Vera's blouse, their hair holding the red light of the sun. Vera calculates the projected angle of the telephone pole's fall. "Look at those guy wires," she says. "They're already pulling it toward the living room."

Megan steps back into the kitchen. George says,

"If we're in the living room when it comes, we'll stand under that door frame."

Megan sighs into the steam of vegetarian tomato sauce and takes shelter under a door frame in her head. George and Vera: for them life is full of definable problems with definable solutions. Don't eat candy, don't smoke cigarettes, don't stand near the window when the earth is quaking.

Vera returns to the kitchen and asks Megan for flour to make the pasta. Vera is not making lasagna, which anybody can make. She is making manicotti stuffed with spinach and cheese, and she is doing it from scratch. George stays in the living room while Megan sits at the kitchen table and watches Vera rub eggs into the flour and roll the dough on the counter into paper-thin sheets. She works vigorously without getting flour on her blue silk blouse. Then she beats four eggs into a bowl of fresh ricotta cheese.

Megan begins to swing her leg and tap her foot. Megan is nervous and Vera is not, but then Vera is on Valium.

George comes into the kitchen, and Vera begins to drop the delicate sheets of pasta into boiling water.

George says, "It sure smells good," and Megan says, "Vera wants to give us the kid, which I think is a crummy idea, what do you think?"

No one says anything.

George moves across the kitchen and leans against the counter and says, finally, "Well, I didn't think we were going to be testy about this whole thing."

Vera says, "We don't have to talk. I thought we'd just eat, and after supper we can talk or not talk."

Megan says, "George, why didn't you think we'd get testy?"

George shakes his head and looks at the linoleum, as if everything is going over his head. Vera looks into the bubbling pot and begins to cry. She dips a slotted spoon into the pot and withdraws a piece of pasta. "Look at it," she says. "It's ruined." The noodle slithers off the spoon and falls to the floor. In the water it has developed large fissures and bursting bubbles. "You gave me self-rising flour, you didn't give me regular," she says. She withdraws another puffed and exploded noodle, which also falls to the floor.

"Think of it as an accident," Megan says. "I couldn't help myself."

Vera continues to cry and spoon noodles out of the pot until the floor looks as though it is piled with glistening rags. Megan watches George and George watches the noodles. Then he kneels and tries to scoop them up and put them back in the pot. "Don't cry," he says. He touches Vera's beautiful blouse with a wet hand. "Don't cry."

Megan stands up, feeling a deep rage in her bones, as if her bones might hurl themselves across the kitchen and fall upon the two of them like clubs. "What about me?" she says. She waits for the rage to pass, and when it doesn't, she sees that handfuls of ricotta cheese are flying across the kitchen. When she sits back down at the table, she says, "All I wanted was not to know."

George has gone to Los Angeles again and Vera is no longer pregnant. Megan drove her to the clinic, waited in the waiting room, smoked cigarettes, sucked lemon drops, bought a ham (nitrite) sandwich from the machine, ate half, threw it away, thought about the transparent tube, the contents dropping into the basin, the basin emptied into the hospital garbage disposal, the copper pipes whooshing it toward the sea. Megan knows where those things go, because she asked about them after her fallopian tube was removed. Aborted fetuses, amputated limbs, benign tumors, everything goes back to the sea, rises into the air again as rain, and falls back to the earth. Not a bad ending if you can think of it that way.

Now as she lies in bed with a book in her lap, the

springs begin to jiggle, the pictures on the wall move against their nails. The apartment groans like a sailing ship. This must be it: the big one. She leaps from the bed and considers the closet, the kitchen table, the door frame near the stairwell. She moves in a circle. She thinks of the gas main. She goes into the living room, and it is over.

Midnight and the local news has covered the quake, a minor tremor, only 5.0 on the scale, worse in high buildings than in low ones, but of no danger to human life. She lies in bed in the dark, feeling safe, feeling giddy, and thinks about the old woman who lives apart from her son on the twelfth floor of the Sunset Tower Senior Home, how she must have stiffened in her bed as the water glasses trembled on the tables, how she must have called out to her roommate, the thief, as the bed moved on its metal wheels, one hundred and twenty feet above the ground. Then Megan slides into sleep, where she may say something strange or terrible, which no one will hear, a message spoken to herself but kept forever secret.

THE BATTLE OF FALLEN TIMBERS

*U*ncle Roofer was a big, friendly, gap-toothed man, a little heavy in the hand-shake, hot-tempered and smiling all at once. He owned a car dealership, a filling station, and a used-car lot. He had once played football for Paul Brown. When they talked about Uncle Roofer's drinking problem, the members of my family always said that Roofer had never got past football. "Once you've played football for Paul Brown, you can't go back to northern Ohio and sell family cars," they said.

Uncle Roofer was a diabetic who drank bourbon.

Uncle Roofer was an alcoholic who ate lithium for lunch.

One day Uncle Roofer and the bourbon and lithium got into the same car and drove to a Browns game in Cleveland. On the way back, they met a concrete retaining wall.

We were living in Oklahoma then and had to fly back to Ohio for the funeral. My grandmother was living

alone in Killbuck, Ohio, at number 7 South Mad Anthony Street. The street was named for General Mad
Anthony Wayne, who had won the Battle of Fallen
Timbers and secured the Northwest Territory against
the Indians so that white settlers could take the land.
When the origin of the street name was explained to me
as a child, I had always got the impression that Mad
Anthony Wayne had fought that battle on behalf of our
family as if the white frame house on South Mad Anthony were already standing above the brick street and
awaiting the arrival of our people from the East.

The year that Uncle Roofer died my grandmother
still had twenty years left of her life and was trying to
figure out whether she could live alone with a bad hip,
held together with steel pins, one leg now three inches
shorter than the other and projecting slightly from her
body at a strange angle. She had to take a bus to get to
the town where my uncle had lived. When I think of her
making that long rocking trip in autumn, over the hills
that held the Killbuck Valley, into the fertile lake plain
up north, when I think of her traveling by bus to the
funeral of her only son, I think of how her leg must have
stuck out into the aisle, of how she must have tried to
pull it close to the seat whenever someone brushed by

on the way to the bathroom. I think of how in her lap was a large black purse, hugged to her body against the sway and saw of the bus. It was late October, and she had brought sugared marshmallow Halloween candy for the grandchildren she would see at the funeral. From time to time, she touched the big purse in her lap and opened it to see if the marshmallow had been squashed during the trip. When we met her at the bus station, she smiled with joy at seeing the living.

"Look here," she said. "I've been thinking of you." She smoothed the cellophane lids of the boxes and handed them to me and my brother, each box containing twelve orange-and-black marshmallow cats. In our hands, we could feel the heat of her body on those boxes. By then my brother and I no longer ate marshmallow cats. We looked at each other with a secret gaze that said we would just have to pretend that we were still young enough to love that sweet-sweet candy, brought so far and with such care, by our grandmother on the day she had come to bury her only son.

After the funeral, we drove my grandmother back to the Killbuck Valley in a Lincoln Continental we borrowed from Roofer's bankrupt dealership. The car had push-button windows and leather seats, which made us feel prosperous. No one mentioned Roofer, his good looks and his promise, his rise and decline, the possibility that his death was a suicide, a form of giving up. Instead, we listened to my father explain the Wisconsin glaciation, how it scoured the topsoil from Canada, gouged out the Great Lakes, and dropped all the good soil exactly where both sides of our family someday were going to live. Everyone nodded and listened and looked appreciatively out the windows, even my grandmother, who still was using two hands to hold the big black purse on her lap. Then my father got to the Ordinance of 1787, which drew straight lines where the roads would be, put a grid across swamps, sliced through hills, walked on water.

"Look at this roadcut," my father said. "Only a man sitting in Washington would draw a road through here."

He was detouring through the valley, taking the long way home, leaving the state road for a county road and a county road for a narrow curving road that followed a creek bed. "Now this road is a different story," my father said. "This road follows an old Indian trail. This road was built by pioneers who had the good sense to read the land."

"I guess you know we're part Indian," my grand-mother said.

"No," my mother said. "What part is that?"

"We're part Wyandot," my grandmother said.

"You never told me," my mother said. "Who was Indian?"

"I'm full of surprises," my grandmother said.

"Was this one of the Indians Mad Anthony Wayne ran out of Ohio?" my brother said.

"It was my great-great grandmother," my grand-mother said.

"I guess she wasn't at the Battle of Fallen Tim-bers," my brother said.

"I don't know much about her," my grandmother said. "She's dead."

"The Wyandots knew how to plan a good road," my father said.

"Nobody ever tells me anything about my own family," my mother said.

"I guess the Battle of Fallen Timbers was sort of like the Civil War," my brother said. "Our own people took the land away from some of our other own people."

"I always thought that it was Roofer who got the Indian blood," my grandmother said.

"The Battle of Fallen Timbers was nothing at all like the Civil War," my father said. "It was a skirmish on the frontier."

"You could see it in his face," my grandmother said. "He had high cheekbones. You could see it in his eyes sometimes."

"He did have high cheekbones," my mother said. "That's what made him so handsome."

Actually, Roofer had had chestnut-red hair and pink skin, an Irish look, but thinking of him as we swung across the valley and saw the tower of the courthouse appear through the trees, I began to think of Roofer as a Wyandot hunting bear and marking trails. There seemed to be agreement all through the car that Roofer had had high cheekbones and might have got the Indian gene my grandmother carried. We were all nodding thoughtfully as we pulled up before number 7 South Mad Anthony and noticed the chipping and alligatored paint on the old house. I knew that my brother and I were going to hurry upstairs to look in the vanity mirror and try to discover whether we looked like Wyandots. We got out of the car in silence and in that moment we concluded forever our family discussion of who Roofer had once been. We consigned him to history, as remote and faint as an old Wyandot trail. In the future, whenever we invoked his name, it would be in a kind of terse code: "Oh, that's the kind of car Roofer used to sell." "That's the kind of play Roofer used to run." These sentences always implied a larger story, but for us, when we were in the company of family, Roofer's story had become untellable.

SNOW ANGEL

*S*ometimes   Marguerite likes to sit in the closet. It's late afternoon and Francis isn't home yet. John and Barbie are on their elbows in front of the TV screen, the casserole's in the oven, the walk's shoveled, there's salt on the driveway, and Marguerite is sitting in the back of the closet on an old feather tick and enjoying the smell of oranges stuck with cloves. This morning there was a blizzard, which kept the children home from school, and when it stopped snowing it was still too cold to let them go out to play.

"Why can't we?"

"You want your feet to turn to ice?" Marguerite said. "You want your nose to fall off?"

First they argued about slap jack, and Barbie screamed because John hit her hand every time she reached for the stack of cards. Then they fought over the talking Kalculating Kat, and John screamed because Barbie lifted the register grille and dropped the Kalculating Kat into the aluminum furnace duct. Barbie had to go to her room for an hour, and John spilled a five-pound sack of flour on the kitchen floor when he tried to make chocolate-butterscotch-raspberry-mint pancakes. Marguerite at the time was in the basement taking apart the aluminum duct. So it went. But now John and Barbie are laughing in front of the TV as cartoon birds are flattened by falling safes and cartoon dogs are blown apart by bombs that look like bowling balls. Marguerite can hear the sounds of wonderful catastrophe coming from the living room. It is good to be upstairs, sitting in the tropical darkness of the closet.

"Hey, Mom!"

What she wanted was a ten-minute snooze of an interlude. Instead she scuffles along under the palmy fringe of hanging pants and the door opens before she can stand up.

"Hi, sweetie," she says to John. "What do you want?"

"What are you doing in the closet?"

"Just looking for an old pair of boots."

"No, you're not." John opens his eyes wide like a storybook wolf. "You're hiding."

"What do you want, honey?"

"I caught you. *You were hiding and I caught you.*"

"Did you want anything in particular, sweetheart?" Marguerite is still on her hands and knees, looking up like a dog at her seven-year-old son.

John frowns with unusual seriousness and says, "You better come quick. Barbie cut off her toe."

"How could you? How could you do this to your own mother?"

The blood is red poster paint, and the amputated toe is a piece of cat dung they pulled out of the litter box. There is a wail in Marguerite's voice, something fierce and primeval. Barbie begins to cry. She rubs paint into her eyes and cries harder.

"I'll get the sponge," says John, already on his way to the kitchen.

"You certainly will."

She takes Barbie up the stairs to the bathroom. Barbie is four years old, not easy to carry anymore. When they get to the landing, Barbie stops crying and says, "Mommy, look what you did."

Marguerite turns around. There is a wiggly red streak, from the bottom of the steps to the landing, where Barbie's painted foot has brushed against the wall. "Fine. Now we've got painted wallpaper to go with our painted carpet."

Marguerite is twenty-nine years old. She is not quite tall, not quite thin, and not quite blond. In high school she played second clarinet in the concert band. In college, she was treasurer of the Environmental Action Society. When she tries to think of the achievements in her life, she can think of nothing to boast about, not even some little thing that it would be pleasing to have slip out at a party. ("I didn't know that Marguerite was a *sky-diver*!")

"The phone," says John. "Daddy."

"Will you go in there with Barbie and see if she can keep her head above water for two minutes?"

Standing by the wall phone in the kitchen, Marguerite looks through the window and watches the wind shake the stiff branches of an oak tree. The snow is gray, the sky is gray, and on the low gray hill that used to be part of a pasture, she can see the skeletal frames of four new houses. When she was a child, her parents' backyard adjoined a small woods where she used to play. The woods is now a shopping mall. The parking lot of the shopping mall is famous for its drug deals.

"Generally a lousy day," Francis is saying, but there are no broken nerve ends in his voice, no frayed tendons. "I'm calling to tell you where I am."

"Acapulco?" she says. "Brazil?"

Francis laughs. "I'm at a place called Mighty Mike's Mobil Station and Auto Parts." Francis loves all gas stations and all auto parts. His voice sounds lush and green even though he is about to describe a car breakdown. He was driving one of the men home from work when the car died at an intersection. They had to push it two blocks to get to Mighty Mike's, but when they got there, the two mechanics were out on calls, so he and the man, Dean Brown, are going to see whether they can fix the car themselves out in the parking lot.

"I'll hold dinner," she says.

"That's okay. We can eat out of the machines here."

"It's lasagna," she says. "It'll still be fine when you get here."

"No, really," he says. "I'll be fine here."

After they hang up, she says to herself, "And how was your day, Marguerite?" "Well," she says to the window. "The cat climbed up the draperies and left a trail of loopy threads all the way to the top. That made my heart beat. The handle fell off the snow shovel that I had purchased at great savings from K-Mart during the Blue Light Special. There was the Kalculating Kat problem, the floor fiasco, and the imaginary missing bloody toe. If I had somebody to tell these things to, I think I could make them into good stories."

Here is the cheerful almost-family scene. John, Barbie, and Marguerite are playing Parcheesi at the kitchen table. Everyone had two helpings of lasagna and no one has a cold. The cat is in the fourth chair, fat and sleepy, seventeen pounds of Kitty Meat Bites. Outside it is dark and the wind skims down the hill and throws puffs of grainy snow at the windows, but here a warm light glows near the yellow walls and begonias bloom red on the windowsill as two children in homemade robes grow sleepy over a Parcheesi board.

"You *cheated,*" John says to Marguerite. "You moved your man eleven spaces and you only rolled a ten."

"Cheater," says Barbie, rocking from side to side in her chair.

"Well, I'll just have to move it back a space," Marguerite says.

"Cheater, meater, feeter," Barbie says.

"No, you lose your turn."

"No, I don't," Marguerite says. "And you know why, sweetie? Because I'm the mother. I made a mistake, I miscounted, and now because I am the mother,

I am moving back eleven spaces, although in a fair and friendly game, I would have to move back only one space." Now the phone is ringing. "All right, I lose a turn."

Francis tells her that Dean Brown's wife has picked them up at the gas station and taken them both to the Browns' house. The Browns have fed him a delicious pot roast (he says this loudly so that the Browns will hear his appreciation) and now they have offered him the sofa for the night, but of course they will drive him home if he really wants them to, but then how would he get to the garage in the morning.

"Weet, beet, keet," Barbie is saying.

Pauline Brown takes the phone and says, "He won't be any trouble, Marguerite." The Browns do not have any children. Marguerite has a momentary vision of their childless house—the high-tech gadgets, the expensive furniture, no dust.

"Teat, eat, sheet."

"Barbie, stop that rocking!" she calls. Too late. The chair slips sideways as Marguerite lunges after it, but Barbie is already on the floor and taking the huge breath that precedes a scream.

"Marguerite?" says Francis from the dangling receiver.

Marguerite scoops Barbie up with one arm and picks up the phone with the other. "Listen, I'll see you tomorrow." Barbie screams. "I don't think any of you should drive on a night like this."

"Everything all right there?"

"Everything is all right. Just a little fall."

Marguerite hangs up and sits on the chair, stroking Barbie's elbow until she stops crying. John says, "You can move eleven spaces if you want to, Mom."

The closet is deep and dark. Behind the clothes, under the shelves that hold shoes and stored linen, there is a niche just large enough for Marguerite and the feather tick. As she follows Barbie upstairs, past the bedroom where the closet is, she thinks of how pleasing it will be to take the satiny comforter from the foot of the double bed and curl up in the niche. The closet smells good. All the closets in the house smell of clove-stuck oranges, the fragrance of her childhood—pomanders made the way her mother used to make them. Floating on the feather tick, she can evoke images of what it was like to be seven, in summer, and reading a book. Or she can be a single woman, in Tahiti, lying in the shade of a coconut palm, the sea breeze lifting the hem of her white dress like butterfly wings.

"No, no," Barbie says. "I. Think. I. Can. Like that." They are lying on Barbie's bed again, against the pillows, while Marguerite reads *The Little Engine That Could.*

"I. Think. I. Can. I. Know. I. Can." Marguerite makes her voice grind out the words slowly as she imitates the sound of a locomotive struggling uphill. Now that she has the rhythms right, she feels Barbie settle into the crook of her arm. "Ithink. Ican. Iknow. Ican." The little engine gathers speed. It goes faster, and faster, and faster, uphill past childhood, youth, middle age, past alcoholism, divorce, the drug addictions of her children, old age on a fixed income, rising prices, drought, floods, blizzards, the cold wind that blows everything away.

"That's enough for tonight," she tells Barbie.

"You put a worm once in Daddy's spaghetti," John says. She has come down to watch the last ten minutes of a program with him. Now during the commercial break, while two hysterical housewives run headlong across a kitchen floor, pushing mops soaked in competing cleansers, John is suggesting that she has no sense of humor. "Daddy thought it was funny," he says. "He didn't scream at you."

"I wasn't mad because you played a joke. I was mad because I thought Barbie was hurt." Besides, there was paint on the carpet, there was paint on the wall. She thinks of Francis sitting down to a hand of hearts and a scotch on the rocks with the Browns. Dear Francis, since you are very far away, I will write you a letter. What I did today: I made pomanders for the closets. Also I went to the big closet twice and just sat there, hunched up, rubbing my shin bones. I hid from my own kids. Some mother, huh? "It *was* a pretty funny joke, John." But John has already turned back to the TV and is laughing at a woman who has just dropped her evening bag into a soup tureen.

"This is not a bad life," she continues. "We have a nice little house, and plenty to eat, and only as many debts as we think we are going to be able to pay. We are doing much better than most people living in the last quarter of the twentieth century."

A deep and unusual silence has slipped into the house. She notices it the moment she flicks the kitchen light and stands near the darkness of the doorway. It is not just the stillness of sleeping children but a special quiet that she realizes has been there for some time, underneath her footsteps as she moved about the house, stacking books and magazines, plumping up pillows. She goes to the back door and looks out. What she has been hearing for three days, without really hearing it, is the wind. The wind blowing swirls of snow down the slope of the back hill, throwing drifts across the driveway, making ridges of ice in the street, where the salted snow melted and refroze. The sound is gone now and there is only the deep silence of snow and of a small full moon high above the stand of trees at the top of the hill. She takes her coat, hat, and muffler from the hook by the door. Except to shovel the walk, she has not been outside for three days.

The snow has frozen over and her feet make soft noises as they break through the thin crust. She walks uphill toward what will be the backyards of four new houses. In the lives of her children the construction of these houses will mark time and change. Her breath rises in frosty puffs, like signals, as she turns to look downhill. There is something serene about the geometry of her neighborhood—the dark rectangle of houses, the snow-glazed roofs. There is no one to see her, although for a moment she imagines that she has been spotted from one of the darkened windows and that a stranger is preparing to send her coded messages, using the flash of a mirror in the moonlight. "Who's there?" she cries in the theatrical voice she used to read Barbie "Three Billy Goats Gruff," but the words slide away into the deepness of the snow and she is not certain that she has spoken.

She walks along the crest of the hill and stops. Behind her there is a curve of footsteps arching along the hill and back down to the house. In front of her there is a large stretch of virgin snow. She takes a leaping giant step forward and then sits down and leans back carefully into the snow, keeping her feet together and her arms by her sides, so that she is lying quite straight and looking up at the soft shadow that curls along the face of the full moon. She begins to move, pushing her arms out across the snow and bringing them up toward her head, then down to her sides. She moves her legs across the snow in a scissors motion— out, then back.

Marguerite, aged twenty-nine, mother of two, is making a snow angel.

In a moment she will be so cold that she will have to stand up and go home. She will have to scuffle around on top of the angel to obliterate the evidence of this whimsy. But now she lies deep in the snow and moves her arms and legs very slowly. She moves with the slow rhythm of the moon moving across the sky. She moves with the slow beat of the stars pulsating their light to stars in other galaxies. She has a pair of white wings and a white skirt. She has white moonlight and the clean white frost of her own breath, and now, alone on the hillside in the white universe, with the shadow of her own footsteps reaching back to the house like a lifeline, Marguerite feels the calm of a great and voluptuous sigh.

*E*very so often that dead dog dreams me up again.

It's twenty-five years later. I'm walking along 42nd Street in Manhattan, the sounds of the city crashing beside me—horns, gearshifts, insults—somebody's chewing gum holding my foot to the pavement, when that dog wakes from his long sleep and imagines me.

I'm sweet again. I'm sweet-breathed and flat-limbed. Our family is stationed at Fort Niagara, and the dog swims his red heavy fur into the black Niagara River. Across the street from the officers' quarters, down the steep shady bank, the river, even this far downstream, has been clocked at nine miles per hour. The dog swims after the stick I have thrown.

"Are you crazy?" my grandmother says, even though she is not fond of dog hair in the house, the way it sneaks into the refrigerator every time you open the door. "There's a current out there! It'll take that dog all the way to Toronto!"

"The dog knows where the backwater ends and the current begins," I say, because it is true. He comes down to the river all the time with my father, my brother MacArthur, or me. You never have to yell the dog away from the place where the river water moves like a whip.

Sparky Smith and I had a game we played called knockout. It involved a certain way of breathing and standing up fast that caused the blood to leave the brain as if a plug had been jerked from the skull. You came to again just as soon as you were on the ground, the blood sloshing back, but it always seemed as if you had left the planet, had a vacation on Mars, and maybe stopped back at Fort Niagara half a lifetime later.

There weren't many kids my age on the post, because it was a small command. Most of its real work went on at the missile batteries flung like shale along the American-Canadian border. Sparky Smith and I hadn't been at Lewiston-Porter Central School long enough to get to know many people, so we entertained ourselves by meeting in a hollow of trees and shrubs at the far edge of the parade ground and telling each other seventh-grade sex jokes that usually had to do with keyholes and doorknobs, hot dogs and hot-dog buns, nuns, priests, preachers, schoolteachers, and people in blind-folds.

When we ran out of sex jokes, we went to knockout and took turns catching each other as we fell like a cut tree toward the ground. Whenever I knocked out, I came to on the grass with the dog barking, yelping, crouching, crying for help. "Wake up! Wake up!" he seemed to say. "Do you know your name? Do you know your name? My name is Duke! My name is Duke!" I'd wake to the sky with the urgent call of the dog in the air, and I'd think, Well, here I am, back in my life again.

Sparky Smith and I spent our school time smiling too much and running for office. We wore mittens instead of gloves, because everyone else did. We made our mothers buy us ugly knit caps with balls on top—caps that in our previous schools would have identified us as weird but were part of the winter uniform in upstate New York. We wobbled onto the ice of the post rink, practicing in secret, banged our knees, scraped the palms of our hands, so that we would be invited to skating parties by civilian children.

"You skate?" With each other we practiced the cool look.

"Oh, yeah. I mean, like, I do it some—I'm not a racer or anything."

Every morning we boarded the Army-green bus—the slime-green, dead-swamp-algae-green bus—and rode it to the post gate, past the concrete island where the MPs stood in their bulletproof booth. Across from the gate, we got off at a street corner and waited with the other Army kids, the junior-high and high-school kids, for the real bus, the yellow one with the civilian kids on it. Just as we began to board, the civilian kids—there were only six of them but eighteen of us—would begin to sing the Artillery song with obscene variations one of them had invented. Instead of "Over hill, over dale," they sang things like "Over boob, over tit." For a few weeks, we sat in silence watching the heavy oak trees of the town give way to apple orchards and potato farms, and we pretended not to hear. Then one day Sparky Smith began to sing the real Artillery song, the booming song with caissons rolling along in it, and we all joined in and took over the bus with our voices.

When we ran out of verses, one of the civilian kids, a football player in high school, yelled, "Sparky is a *dog's* name. Here Sparky, Sparky, Sparky." Sparky rose from his seat with a wounded look, then dropped to the aisle on his hands and knees and bit the football player in the calf. We all laughed, even the football player, and Sparky returned to his seat.

"That guy's just lucky I didn't pee on his leg," Sparky said.

Somehow Sparky got himself elected homeroom president and me homeroom vice president in January. He liked to say, "In actual percentages—I mean in actual per capita terms—we are doing much better than the civilian kids." He kept track of how many athletes we had, how many band members, who among the older girls might become a cheerleader. Listening to him even then, I couldn't figure out how he got anyone to vote for us. When he was campaigning, he sounded dull and serious, and anyway he had a large head and looked funny in a knit cap. He put up a homemade sign in the lunchroom, went from table to table to find students from 7-B to shake hands with, and said to me repeatedly, as I walked along a step behind and nodded, "Just don't tell them that you're leaving in March. Under no circumstances let them know that you will not be able to finish out your term."

In January, therefore, I was elected homeroom vice president by people I still didn't know (nobody in 7-B rode our bus—that gave us an edge), and in March my family moved to Fort Sill, in Oklahoma. I surrendered my vice presidency to a civilian girl, and that was the end for all time of my career in public office.

Two days before we left Fort Niagara, we took the dog, Duke, to Charlie Battery, fourteen miles from the post, and left him with the mess sergeant. We were leaving him for only six weeks, until we could settle in Oklahoma and send for him. He had stayed at Charlie Battery before, when we visited our relatives in Ohio at Christmastime. He knew there were big meaty bones at Charlie Battery, and scraps of chicken, steak, turkey, slices of cheese, special big-dog bowls of ice cream. The mess at Charlie Battery was Dog Heaven, so he gave us a soft, forgiving look as we walked with him from the car to the back of the mess hall.

My mother said, as she always did at times like that, "I wish he knew more English." My father gave him a fierce manly scratch behind the ear. My brother and I scraped along behind with our pinched faces.

"Don't you worry," the sergeant said. "He'll be fine here. We like this dog, and he likes us. He'll run that fence perimeter all day long. He'll be his own early-warning defense system. Then we'll give this dog everything he ever dreamed of eating." The sergeant looked quickly at my father to see if the lighthearted reference to the defense system had been all right. My father was in command of the missile batteries. In my father's presence, no one spoke lightly of the defense of the United States of America—of the missiles that would rise from the earth like a wind and knock out (knock out!) the Soviet planes flying over the North Pole with their nuclear bombs. But Duke was my father's dog, too, and I think that my father had the same wish we all had—to tell him that we were going to send for him, this was just going to be a wonderful dog vacation.

"Sergeant Mozley has the best mess within five hundred miles," my father said to me and MacArthur.

We looked around. We had been there for Thanksgiving dinner when the grass was still green. Now, in late winter, it was a dreary place, a collection of rain-streaked metal buildings standing near huge dark mounds of earth. In summer, the mounds looked something like the large grassy mounds in southern Ohio, the famous Indian mounds, softly rounded and benignly mysterious. In March, they were black with old snow. Inside the mounds were the Nike missiles, I supposed, although I didn't know for sure where the missiles were. Perhaps they were hidden in the depressions behind the mounds.

...

Once during "Fact Monday" in Homeroom 7-B, our teacher, Miss Bintz, had given a lecture on nuclear weapons. First she put a slide on the wall depicting an atom and its spinning electrons.

"Do you know what this is?" she said, and everyone in the room said, "An atom," in one voice, as if we were reciting a poem. We liked "Fact Monday" sessions because we didn't have to do any work for them. We sat happily in the dim light of her slides through lectures called "Nine Chapters in the Life of a Cheese" ("First the milk is warmed, then it is soured with rennet"), "The Morning Star of English Poetry" ("As springtime suggests the beginning of new life, so Chaucer stands at the beginning of English poetry"), and "Who's Who Among the Butterflies" ("The monarch—*Danaus plexippus*—is king"). Sparky liked to say that Miss Bintz was trying to make us into third-graders again, but I liked Miss Bintz. She had high cheekbones and a passionate voice. She believed, like the adults in my family, that a fact was something solid and useful, like a penknife you could put in your pocket in case of emergency.

That day's lecture was "What Happens to the Atom When It Is Smashed." Miss Bintz put on the wall a black-and-white slide of four women who had been horribly disfigured by the atomic blast at Hiroshima.

The room was half darkened for the slide show. When she surprised us with the four faces of the women, you could feel the darkness grow, the silence in the bellies of the students.

"And do you know what this is?" Miss Bintz said. No one spoke. What answer could she have wanted from us, anyway? She clicked the slide machine through ten more pictures—close-ups of blistered hands, scarred heads, flattened buildings, burned trees, maimed and naked children staggering toward the camera as if the camera were food, a house, a mother, a father, a friendly dog.

"Do you know what this is?" Miss Bintz said again. Our desks were arranged around the edge of the room, creating an arena in the center. Miss Bintz entered that space and began to move along the front of our desks, looking to see who would answer her incomprehensible question.

"Do you know?" She stopped in front of my desk.

"No," I said.

"Do you know?" She stopped next at Sparky's desk.

Sparky looked down and finally said, "It's something horrible."

"That's right," she said. "It's something very horrible. This is the effect of an atom smashing. This is the effect of nuclear power." She turned to gesture at the slide, but she had stepped in front of the projector, and the smear of children's faces fell across her back. "Now let's think about how nuclear power got from the laboratory to the scientists to the people of Japan." She had begun to pace again. "Let's think about where all this devastation and wreckage actually comes from. You tell me," she said to a large crouching boy named Donald Anderson. He was hunched over his desk, and his arms lay before him like tree limbs.

"I don't know," Donald Anderson said.

"Of course you do," Miss Bintz said. "Where did all of this come from?"

None of us had realized yet that Miss Bintz's message was political. I looked beyond Donald Anderson at the drawn window shades. Behind them were plate-glass windows, a view of stiff red-oak leaves, the smell of wood smoke in the air. Across the road from the school was an orchard, beyond that a pasture, another orchard, and then the town of Lewiston, standing on the Niagara River seven miles upstream from the long row of red-brick Colonial houses that were the officers' quarters at Fort Niagara. Duke was down the river, probably sniffing at the reedy edge, his head lifting when ducks flew low over the water. Once the dog had come back to our house with a live fish in his mouth, a carp. Nobody ever believed that story except those of us who saw it: me, my mother and father and brother, my grandmother.

Miss Bintz had clicked to a picture of a mushroom cloud and was now saying, "And where did the bomb come from?" We were all tired of "Fact Monday" by then. Miss Bintz walked back to where Sparky and I were sitting. "You military children," she said. "You know where the bomb comes from. Why don't you tell us?" she said to me.

Maybe because I was tired, or bored, or frightened—I don't know—I said to Miss Bintz, looking her in the eye, "The bomb comes from the mother bomb."

Everyone laughed. We laughed because we needed to laugh, and because Miss Bintz had all the answers and all the questions and she was pointing them at us like guns.

"Stand up," she said. She made me enter the arena in front of the desks, and then she clicked the machine back to the picture of the Japanese women. "Look at this picture and make a joke," she said. What came next was the lecture she had been aiming for all along. The bomb came from the United States of America. We in the United States were worried about whether another country might use the bomb, but in the whole history of the human species only one country had ever used the worst weapon ever invented. On she went, bombs and airplanes and bomb tests, and then she got to the missiles. They were right here, she said, not more than ten miles away. Didn't we all know that? "You know that, don't you?" she said to me. If the missiles weren't hidden among our orchards, the planes from the Soviet Union would not have any reason to drop bombs on top of Lewiston-Porter Central School.

I had stopped listening by then and realized that the pencil I still held in my hand was drumming a song against my thigh. Over hill, over dale. I looked back at the wall again, where the mushroom cloud had reappeared, and my own silhouette stood wildly in the middle of it. I looked at Sparky and dropped the pencil on the floor, stooped down to get it, looked at Sparky once more, stood up, and knocked out.

Later, people told me that I didn't fall like lumber, I fell like something soft collapsing, a fan folding in on itself, a balloon rumpling to the floor. Sparky saw what I was up to and tried to get out from behind his desk to catch me, but it was Miss Bintz I fell against, and she went down, too. When I woke up, the lights were on, the mushroom cloud was a pale ghost against the wall, voices in the room sounded like insect wings, and I was back in my life again.

"I'm so sorry," Miss Bintz said. "I didn't know you were an epileptic."

At Charlie Battery, it was drizzling as my parents stood and talked with the sergeant, rain running in dark tiny ravines along the slopes of the mounds.

MacArthur and I had M&M's in our pockets, which we were allowed to give to the dog for his farewell. When we extended our hands, though, the dog lowered himself to the gravel and looked up at us from under his tender red eyebrows. He seemed to say that if he took the candy he knew we would go, but if he didn't perhaps we would stay here at the missile battery and eat scraps with him.

We rode back to the post in silence, through gray apple orchards, through small upstate towns, the fog rising out of the rain like a wish. MacArthur and I sat against opposite doors in the back seat, thinking of the loneliness of the dog.

We entered the kitchen, where my grandmother had already begun to clean the refrigerator. She looked at us, at our grim children's faces—the dog had been sent away a day earlier than was really necessary—and she said, "Well, God knows you can't clean the dog hair out of the house with the dog still in it."

Whenever I think of an Army post, I think of a place the weather cannot touch for long. The precise rectangles of the parade grounds, the precisely pruned trees and shrubs, the living quarters, the administration buildings, the PX and commissary, the nondenominational church, the teen club, snack bar, the movie house, the skeet-and-trap field, the swimming pools, the runway, warehouses, the officers' club, the NCO club. Men marching, women marching, saluting, standing at attention, at ease. The bugle will trumpet reveille, mess call, assembly, retreat, taps through a hurricane, a tornado, flood, blizzard. Whenever I think of the clean squared look of a military post, I think that if one were blown down today in a fierce wind, it would be standing again tomorrow in time for reveille.

The night before our last full day at Fort Niagara, an arctic wind slipped across the lake and froze the rain where it fell, on streets, trees, power lines, rooftops. We awoke to a fabulation of ice, the sun shining like a weapon, light rocketing off every surface except the surfaces of the Army's clean streets and walks.

MacArthur and I stood on the dry, scraped walk in front of our house and watched a jeep pass by on the way to the gate. On the post, everything was operational, but in the civilian world beyond the gate power lines were down, hanging like daggers in the sun, roads were glazed with ice, cars were in ditches, highways were impassible. No yellow school buses were going to be on the roads that morning.

"This means we miss our very last day in school," MacArthur said. "No good-byes for us."

We looked up at the high, bare branches of the hard maples, where drops of ice glimmered.

"I just want to shake your hand and say so long," Sparky said. He had come out of his house to stand with us. "I guess you know this means you'll miss the surprise party."

"There was going to be a party?" I said.

"Just cupcakes," Sparky said. "I sure wish you could stay the school year and keep your office."

"Oh, who cares!" I said, suddenly irritated with Sparky, although he was my best friend. "Jesus," I said, sounding to myself like an adult—like Miss Bintz maybe, when she was off duty. "Jesus," I said again. "What kind of office is home-goddamn-room vice president in a crummy country school?"

MacArthur said to Sparky, "What kind of cupcakes were they having?"

I looked down at MacArthur and said, "Do you
know how totally ridiculous you look in that knit cap?
I can't wait until we get out of this place."

"Excuse me," MacArthur said. "Excuse me for
wearing the hat you gave me for my birthday."

It was then that the dog came back. We heard him
calling out before we saw him, his huge woof-woof. "My
name is Duke! My name is Duke! I'm your dog! I'm your
dog!" Then we saw him streaking through the trees,
through the park space of oaks and maples between our
house and the post gate. Later the MPs would say that
he stopped and wagged his tail at them before he passed
through the gate, as if he understood that he should be
stopping to show his I.D. card. He ran to us, bounding
across the crusted, glass-slick snow—ran into the history of our family, all the stories we would tell about him
after he was dead. Years and years later, whenever we
came back together at the family dinner table, we would
start the dog stories. He was the dog who caught the live
fish with his mouth, the one who stole a pound of butter
off the commissary loading dock and brought it to us in
his soft bird dog's mouth without a tooth mark on the
package. He was the dog who broke out of Charlie

Battery the morning of an ice storm, traveled fourteen miles across the needled grasses and frozen pastures, through the prickly frozen mud of orchards, across backyard fences in small towns, and found the lost family.

The day was good again. When we looked back at the ice we saw a fairyland. The red-brick houses looked like ice castles. The ice-coated trees, with their million dreams of light, seemed to cast a spell over us.

"This is for you," Sparky said, and handed me a gold-foiled box. Inside were chocolate candies and a note that said, "I have enjoyed knowing you this year. I hope you have a good life." Then it said, "P.S. Remember this name. Someday I'm probably going to be famous."

"Famous as what?" MacArthur said.

"I haven't decided yet," Sparky said.

We had a party. We sat on the front steps of our quarters, Sparky, MacArthur, the dog, and I, and we ate all the chocolates at eight o'clock in the morning. We sat shoulder to shoulder, the four of us, and looked across the street through the trees at the river, and we talked about what we might be doing a year from then. Finally, we finished the chocolates and stopped talking and allowed the brilliant light of that morning to enter us.

. . .

Miss Bintz is the one who sent me the news about Sparky four months later. BOY DROWNS IN SWIFT CURRENT. In the newspaper story, Sparky takes the bus to Niagara Falls with two friends from Lewiston-Porter. It's a searing July day, a hundred degrees in the city, so the boys climb down the gorge into the river and swim in a place where it's illegal to swim, two miles downstream from the Falls. The boys Sparky is tagging along with—they're both student-council members as well as football players, just the kind of boys Sparky himself wants to be—have sneaked down to this swimming place many times: a cove in the bank of the river, where the water is still and glassy on a hot July day, not like the water raging in the middle of the river. But the current is a wild invisible thing, unreliable, whipping out with a looping arm to pull you in. "He was only three feet in front of me," one of the boys said. "He took one more stroke and then he was gone."

We were living in civilian housing not far from the post. When we had the windows open, we could hear the bugle calls and the sound of the cannon firing retreat at sunset. A month after I got the newspaper clipping about Sparky, the dog died. He was killed, along with every other dog on our block, when a stranger drove down our street one evening and threw poisoned hamburger into our front yards.

All that week I had trouble getting to sleep at night. One night I was still awake when the recorded bugle sounded taps, the sound drifting across the Army fences and into our bedrooms. Day is done, gone the sun. It was the sound of my childhood in sleep. The bugler played it beautifully, mournfully, holding fast to the long, high notes. That night I listened to the cadence of it, to the yearning of it. I thought of the dog again, only this time I suddenly saw him rising like a missile into the air, the red glory of his fur flying, his nose pointed heavenward. I remembered the dog leaping high, prancing on his hind legs the day he came back from Charlie Battery, the dog rocking back and forth, from front legs to hind legs, dancing, sliding across the ice of the post rink later that day, as Sparky, MacArthur, and I played crack-the-whip, holding tight to each other, our skates careening and singing. "You're AWOL! You're AWOL!" we cried at the dog. "No school!" the dog barked back. "No school!" We skated across the darkening ice into the sunset, skated faster and faster, until we seemed to rise together into the cold, bright air. It was a good day, it was a good day, it was a good day.

ABOUT THE AUTHOR

$\mathcal{S}$TEPHANIE VAUGHN was born in Millersburg, Ohio. She grew up in Ohio, New York, Oklahoma, Texas, the Philippine Islands, and Italy. She was educated at Ohio State University, the University of Iowa, and Stanford University. Currently, she lives in Ithaca, New York.